Pearl's Will

Lockets & Lace
Book 9

Sophie Dawson

DEDICATION

This book is dedicated to
the hard-working authors of the Sweet Americana
Sweethearts blog who provide the world with sweet/clean
historical romances about North Americans between 1820
and 1929.

ACKNOWLEDGMENTS

This book is part of a multi-author series sponsored by the authors who write for the Sweet Americana Sweethearts blog. My appreciation and thanks go to the other authors who helped develop the Lockets & Lace series of books.

I offer my appreciation to Carpe Librum Book Covers for the cover design for my novel.

I thank Zina Abbott for allowing me to be part of this series.

DISCLAIMER

DESCRIPTION

Will Miller doesn't know what to think when the lovely young woman faints in his jewelry and watch repair shop-- except he wants to help her any way he can.

Widow Pearl Ward, struggling to survive, needs to sell the watch-locket given to her on her eighteenth birthday.

When he learns she's expecting, he proposes.

Will Pearl's feelings for her late husband stand between them? Can they build a life together with his mother dead set against them?

MY LOCKET

When I was asked to participate in the Lockets and Lace series I knew I had to do it. First, the Bavarian Jewelry and Watch Shop is set in St. Joseph, Missouri. I was born in St. Joe and my father's family lived there. We moved when I was two but it's still the place where I was born.

Second, is the locket. My grandmother was given a watch-locket pin on her eighteenth birthday by her parents. Engraved on the back cover is *To Pearl Henry, Love Papa and Mama Sept. 9, 1906.* I have that locket. I have had it modified to be a necklace rather than a pin to work with modern clothing and I wear it on special occasions. It still works and is a wonderful way to remember a woman I loved very much.

Pearl's Will

AUTHOR NOTES

The Edwardian era which ended in 1910 was a new timeframe for me so I did quite a lot of research. I was surprised with what I found out. You'll find products in the story you never knew were this old. I'm not going to share them here. Just know that all references to them are correct for 1910. One thing I will note is that at the time Ford Model-T automobiles did come in colors other than black. It wasn't until 1914 when Henry Ford was developing the assembly line to make automobiles available to the genera public that they changed to all black. This was not because he didn't like other colors, but it was cheaper to make them all one color.

CHAPTER ONE

St. Joseph, Missouri
April 1910

Pearl Ward looked up at the cloud covered sky as she hurried along the street. She dearly hoped it wouldn't begin to rain as she hadn't thought to bring an umbrella along. Hunger made thinking difficult and to plan ahead. If her errand was successful she'd be able to purchase food for the upcoming days.

She looked down at the object clutched in her hand, her heart breaking at the thought of selling the watch-locket she'd received from her parents on her eighteenth birthday. It would be four years ago in a few months. September. It was late April now. So much had happened since that lovely day. So much happiness and joy, tragedy and sorrow.

Pearl glanced at the street as the electric trolley went by. It would have made the trip to the Bavarian Jewelry and Watch Repair Shop much easier, but since there was no money for food there certainly weren't coins for the trolley. Her empty belly cramped as she turned the corner. Just another block. The shop was on the corner.

"Please, Lord, let them buy my locket. I don't know what I'll do if they don't. Thank you for your provision of the job at the mercantile. I just need to be able to get through this next week until I'm paid. Just until next

11

Friday. Please, please, Lord," Pearl mumbled her prayer as she dodged the others going about their business on the Saturday morning.

Stopping outside the shop, Pearl opened the watch side of the locket. Yes, it was running. She'd wound it last night before she climbed into her lonely bed.

Closing the cover, being careful not to crush the thin crystal, she opened the back to read the inscription one last time. Tears glistened and nearly slipped down her cheeks, but Pearl blinked them away. There was no help for it. She had to sell the watch or she'd starve. Lifting her head in an effort to feel more confident and brave, Pearl went to the door, opened it, and walked inside, stopping just past the entrance.

The shop was well lit with electric lights and by the windows that flanked the door she had just entered which cut across the corner of the building. On both windows was painted the name of the shop. Though it wasn't turning there was a ceiling fan that would provide circulation in the summer. Several oak framed glass cases displayed watches and jewelry. To the rear of the shop behind a counter with more cases on both ends there was a large workbench. Shelves and cubbies rose above the bench giving space for tools and the parts used to repair watches and create custom jewelry. Pressed tin decorated the ceiling.

"Good morning. How may I help you?"

Pearl quit her perusal of the shop's interior and took in the young man who'd risen from the workbench and come to the counter. He was lean and just slightly above average height. Wavy blonde hair, just long enough to fall over his forehead brought out the silver within the blue eyes. A dark blue bibbed apron covered his white shirt and there were black garters on his upper arms holding back his sleeves.

Pearl took a couple of steps further into the shop.

"Um, yes, I hope so." Now that it was finally time to offer her locket, Pearl found it was much more difficult than she'd anticipated. The watch-locket represented so many aspects of her life that she'd lost. To have to sell it tore a hole in her heart and ripped the scabs off the hurts and pain she'd gone through so recently.

Steeling herself, Pearl walked up to the counter where the man was patiently waiting. "I…" Pearl cleared her throat of the lump lodged there. "I'm wanting to sell my watch-locket. I was told you will purchase jewelry and watches."

"We do at times." When she didn't offer the piece, the man said, "May I see what you've brought?"

"Oh, yes." Pearl set the locket into his outstretched hand.

The jeweler stepped back to the workbench, picked up his jeweler's loop, and began inspecting the watch-locket. Pearl stepped over to a case that flanked the counter. Seeing what was displayed, she laid her hand, fingers spread wide, on the glass.

Inside were several pieces of handmade lace. There were collars and lace edged-handkerchiefs. Pearl leaned down and studied them. When she saw the prices listed on the tags, she closed her hand into a fist. Her lace was of higher quality than these. She glanced at the jeweler. Would he be interested in her lace? Would he consider selling hers as he did these? If he would, maybe she wouldn't have to sell the locket.

~~~~~

Will Miller opened the back of the locket and sighed. The engraving lessened the value. The piece was high quality. The cover over the watch was decorated with a five lobed clover design surrounded by scrolling. In the clover was a thin-pointed star with a small diamond in the center. The back cover repeated the design without the stone. Inside

13

the back cover where a photograph could be placed was an engraving. *'To Pearl Henry, From Papa and Mama, Sept. 9, 1906.'*

Will glanced at the woman who was looking intently into the lace display. She was quite thin, honey blonde hair peeked out from under her wide-brimmed hat. She was wearing the simple clothing of a working woman. Navy skirt with a matching double-breasted long jacket, white blouse with a crocheted lace collar that spread beautifully over the blue. What he could see of her face showed a slim nose, unlike his fairly broad one. He'd have to see what color her eyes were. She lifted her hand and touched the glass of the case. A lace glove encased her slim fingers.

Will looked back at the watch-locket. It was suspended from a gold bow-shaped pin. It would look lovely on the bodice of her jacket. He wondered why she was wanting to sell it. The quality of her clothing wasn't high-society, but it was well tailored and didn't look worn.

Standing, Will moved back to the counter. She came over, waiting with a hopeful expression on her face. Her eyes were a deep green, nearly the color of pine needles. Framed with long lashes, they spoke of sadness, despair, loneliness, and desperation.

Even though Will knew what the true value of the watch-locket was, something told him to offer more. He wouldn't tell his father he paid more for it. He'd pay for it up with his own money.

"Miss? Are you sure you want to sell this? It must have great sentimental value to you."

She looked down a moment, then lifted her eyes again. They glittered with moisture. "Yes, but, if it's possible, and I'll understand if you can't do it, would there be any chance I could purchase it back in the future?"

She must have fallen on extremely hard times. It firmed his intention to help her. It wasn't because she was lovely, Will assured himself. Well, maybe it was a little. He hoped that wasn't his main motivation. His Christian ethic called for being a Good Samaritan for others.

Will set the watch on the counter and named the amount he would pay her for the locket. She lifted a trembling hand to her lips. "I'll hold it back from display so you can redeem it. At least, I can for several months. Would that work for you?"

"Thank you. You're most generous. I'll try to redeem it as soon as I can."

Will picked up the locket and placed it on the workbench. Rather than pay her from the cash register, he opened his personal cash drawer and counted out the bills. He put the locket into the drawer, near the back.

As he turned around to go back to the counter, he saw the woman lay one hand on the counter. The other she raised to her forehead. Then, she collapsed to the floor.

Will ran to the back stairs, opened the door, and yelled for his sister. "Lillian, I need your help." Hoping she heard him, Will ran to the woman now lying in a crumpled heap.

"Miss? Miss?" He patted her cheek. She didn't respond. Relief flooded through him as he heard his sister running down the stairs.

"Will, where are you? What's happened?"

"Out here. This woman fainted. She was standing by the counter and just went down."

"Well, we can't help her here. Pick her up and carry her upstairs. You can put her on the davenport."

Will did as instructed, noting how thin and light his burden was. Once she was on the davenport, Lillian pulled the pins from her hat, placing them, and it, on the end table. Then, she took off the gloves.

"You unbutton her shoes and take them off. My hook is on my dressing table. Get it." She moved to the woman's side and began unbuttoning the jacket. "Who is she?"

"I don't know," Will said as he went to fetch the hook. When he came back he said, "She came in wanting to sell her watch-locket." He didn't mention he'd bought it. He unbuttoned and removed her shoes.

The woman turned her head from side to side and gave a small moan.

"Miss, Miss," Lillian said, patting the hand she was holding.

The eyes Will had noted were so green opened. The woman jerked.

"What? What happened?" She looked from Lillian to Will and back.

"You fainted. Will carried you up here. Do you know why?" Lillian asked.

The woman raised a hand to her forehead. "It may be because I haven't eaten since yesterday morning. I only had a slice of bread then."

"Oh my. Will, get a glass of milk. That will be a good start. I'm Lillian Miller. He's my brother, Will. You're in our flat above the shop. Who are you?"

"Pearl Ward."

"Why haven't you eaten?"

"No money to buy food. Not until I get paid on Friday."

"Oh, honey. That's why you fainted." Lillian gently touched Miss Ward's face.

Will came back with the glass of milk and a plate with buttered bread. He set them on the coffee table. "Do you think you can sit up?"

"I think so."

When she was upright, Will gave her the milk. She took a long drink. "Thank you. You are most generous."

"It's nothing." Will passed her the plate. "Eat this."

"It is when you don't have any food or any way to purchase it."

Will nodded.

All three were quiet while she ate the bread and finished the glass of milk. Will was at a loss as to what to do or say. He looked at Lillian, hoping she knew. As usual, she came through for him.

"Miss Ward. Will you let me fix you some breakfast? I can fry up some bacon and eggs real quick-like. I don't want you leaving here without filling your stomach."

Indecision flashed across the pale face. "I hate to put you out. I'm beholden to you as it is."

"I believe it's Mrs. Ward, Lillian," Will said, looking at the young woman. "I read the engraving on your locket. Your maiden name was Henry, wasn't it?"

"Yes."

Lillian glanced between them. "Why isn't your husband making sure you eat?"

"He passed away twelve days ago after several weeks of illness. He hadn't worked all that time so there was no money coming in. Doctor bills and then the funeral and cemetery plot took what little savings we had. I had to pawn my wedding ring to pay next month's rent."

"Oh, you poor thing. How sad." Lillian put a comforting arm around Mrs. Ward.

"I got a job at Townsend & Wyatt Dry Goods as a sales clerk. They only pay every two weeks. I have until next Friday before I get my first pay."

"And you ran out of food." Lillian stood. "I'm going to fix you that breakfast. I won't take any argument."

Will chuckled. "You sound just like Mother."

"Well, sometimes she's right." Lillian went to the kitchen.

Will and Mrs. Ward looked at each other, neither knowing what to say. She bit her lip. It brought color to the pale skin.

"Mr. Miller. Um, I saw the beautiful lace you had for sale. I was wondering, um, if you take lace on consignment?"

Will looked at her, then picked up one of the gloves lying on the table. "Did you make these?"

"Yes, my collar, too. It's Irish crochet lace. I have several other pieces I could bring to show you. That is, if you are interested."

"Will, where are you? Why aren't you in the shop? The door's unlocked. Do you want everything stolen?"

Will glanced at the stairs. "That's Mother." He rose, crossed the room, and said, "I'm sorry. We had a crisis and I forgot to go lock the shop."

He stepped back when his mother reached the top of the stairs so she could enter the room.

CHAPTER TWO

Pearl looked on as Mr. Miller greeted his mother. She could tell where he got his blonde hair. Mrs. Miller had placed her stamp on Lillian too. The blonde hair, blue eyes, strong chin and determined air was shared by both.

"What's crisis enough that you left the shop untended?"

"Mrs. Ward fainted. We brought her up here to recover," Mr. Miller said.

Mrs. Miller came over and looked down at Pearl. "Why'd she faint?"

"Mrs. Ward has fallen on bad times. She hasn't eaten in over a day."

Pearl was relieved to see some sympathy come into the older woman's eyes.

"Lillian's making her breakfast."

"That's good." Mrs. Miller sat in a sewing chair opposite Pearl. "I'm Mrs. Luella Miller. What's happened to bring you such troubles?"

Before Pearl could answer, Will related what she'd told him and his sister. She noticed he didn't mention the locket and wondered why. He emphasized how she had taken a job so soon after her husband's death and that she'd pawned her ring to pay the rent. When he told of the Irish lace, Mrs. Miller's eyes went to Pearl's collar then she picked up the gloves.

"You do very good work. These gloves match perfectly.

Not all do."

"Thank you. My grandmother taught me. She came from Ireland." Pearl smiled at the memory. "She was very exacting."

"Here's breakfast." Lillian came in carrying a tray with a plate filled with food. "Hello, Mother. I see you've met our waif."

"Yes. Did you make enough?" Mrs. Miller examined the plate.

Lillian placed the tray on Pearl's lap. There was a large serving of scrambled eggs, several slices of bacon, and two pieces of buttered toast. A small dish of raspberry jam and another glass of milk were also on the tray. The plate sat on a rectangular lace doily.

Pearl bowed her head and thanked God for these generous people and for the food they were giving her. The amount of food was more than she normally ate, but she didn't stop eating until every morsel was gone. It tasted delicious and she mentioned that fact several times while she ate. Mrs. Miller beamed when Pearl commented on how wonderful the jam was.

Mr. Miller had gone down to the shop shortly after Pearl began eating. Lillian sat beside her.

"We sell quite a lot of lace in the shop. Mostly collars, handkerchiefs, and gloves. Some doilies and antimacassars, also. Your pieces would sell very well, I think. Do you have any new pieces you could bring in? Ones you've made but haven't used?"

"I made several things while Patrick was ill. Crocheting helps me deal with difficult things. It helps me relax."

"When you feel up to it, bring them in. We can discuss what they will sell for when you do."

Pearl bit her lip. "Would this afternoon be too soon? I work weekdays at Townsend and Wyatt. I couldn't get here until after work."

"Are you sure you feel up to it?" Lillian asked, placing a

hand on Pearl's arm.

"I'll be fine. I need to. It's too long until I can get back here."

"I'll give you trolley money, Mrs. Ward," Mrs. Miller said.

"Oh, you mustn't. You all have been more than generous."

"How about you pay me back from your first sale?" Mrs. Miller smiled at her.

"Thank you." Pearl stood, then sat down again. "My shoes? Where are my shoes?"

Lillian laughed. "Here." She fished them out from under the davenport. "Will took them off."

"What?" Mrs. Miller's tone was scandalized.

"Mother, relax. He didn't see anything other than her stocking feet."

"Still, it's quite improper."

Lillian grinned at her mother, while Pearl buttoned her shoes. "I won't tell anyone if you won't."

"Lillian, really," huffed her mother.

$\sim\sim\sim\sim\sim$

Will stood next to his mother while she inspected the lace items Mrs. Ward had brought in. He hoped they met with her approval since he wanted to help the young widow as much as possible. If they carried her work in the shop, she would be coming in on a fairly regular basis.

"These are lovely, Mrs. Ward. I do believe they will sell well." His mother laid the final piece she'd been looking at on the counter. She went on to explain what each could sell for and how much the commission would be. "Normally, I pay for items after they sell. I'd like to help you out by purchasing these outright. Then, we can begin the commissions after they've sold with the next pieces you bring in."

"Again, you are more generous than I deserve. Thank you."

"Nonsense, my dear. If we can't help others, how do we demonstrate our faith?"

Will looked at his mother. She never failed to surprise him. She could be condescending, judgmental, and abrupt one moment. The next she would be generous, loving, and sweet. It seemed that today she was in the loving mood.

"Will, write up a receipt to record the purchase and start a ledger page for Mrs. Ward. Then pay her for the lacework. I need to get back to your father. He's feeling poorly again. That's why I came in the first place. To let you know he wouldn't be in today."

"Do you think it's serious?" Will asked.

"No more than usual. I tried to get him to allow me to contact a physician, but he won't. I don't know what to do other than let him rest."

"You go to him now, Mother. Assure him I will be fine without him looking over my shoulder." Will grinned at his mother. "He taught me well."

Will kissed his mother's cheek and helped her don her coat. Once she left, he turned to Mrs. Ward. "You do make lovely lace. Much better than some we have carried. I wouldn't be surprised if you are offered commissions. I'll get the money for these."

Will filled out the receipt and opened the ledger to a blank page. After writing her name at the top he listed the items she had brought and what price was paid. "When you bring in some work I'll record each piece, what the commission will be, and the selling price we will list it for. When it sells, I'll mark that, and again when you are paid." He pointed to each column as he moved across the page writing in the headings. Will saw that she was paying close attention.

He counted out the bills and handed them to her. "Do you have enough money to purchase what you need to eat until you are paid next Friday?"

She folded the bills and put them in her handbag. "Yes,

I went to the market on my way home and bought what I will need for the next few days with the money you paid me for the watch-locket before I left earlier. Thank you." She looked as if she wanted to say something else, so Will remained silent. "Mr. Miller. Why didn't you tell your mother about purchasing my locket?"

Will cleared his throat and ran a finger around his stiff collar. "I, ah, purchased your locket with personal funds rather than those of the shop. Since it wasn't money from the business, it was none of her business." He grinned, hoping she caught the pun.

She smiled slightly. "I'm not sure why you did so, used your personal funds, but thank you. I'm not sure how I can repay your kindness. That of your sister and mother, also."

"You don't need to. Not to us. You help someone else in need sometime. Scripture says what you do for the least of these…" He let the sentence drop.

"I will." She smiled and turned to leave.

"When do you think you'll bring more lace?" Will was reluctant to have her leave.

She looked back at him. "If I can get more thread on Monday, I should be able to bring a few small pieces in next Saturday."

"Do you need money to purchase the thread?"

She patted her handbag. "No, I have enough now."

Will watched as she left the shop and walked past the window.

CHAPTER THREE

Pearl rode the trolley to the watch shop the following Saturday. She had a brown paper wrapped bundle in her lap with lace collars, doilies, and lace edged handkerchiefs to deliver. There was also a pair of gloves.

Lillian Miller had come into Townsend and Wyatt Dry Goods on Thursday and found Pearl in the fabric department where she worked. She had hugged Pearl, trying to contain her excitement.

"I just had to come and tell you. We sold all your lace. Mother is delighted. She's hoping you will bring more in this week. She wants to talk with you about some larger items. Something that will show your talents more."

Pearl was shocked. She'd only hoped a few of her pieces would sell. To have them all be sold was astounding. "How wonderful, Miss Miller. I have some finished and was planning to bring them Saturday. Will that be soon enough? I don't know how I would be able to bring them sooner."

"Oh, call me Lillian, and may I call you Pearl? I have a feeling we are going to be very close friends. Yes, Saturday is fine. I was just so pleased when I sold the last collar, I simply had to come and tell you."

"Mrs. Ward, please don't be chatting with friends while you are on duty." It was Mr. Dimmick, her manager. He stepped from behind her.

"Oh, I'm going to be purchasing something. Don't

worry, sir," Lillian said. "I'm wanting to make a summer outfit and need several yards of white dress goods. Lawn, I think. I see you have some here." Lillian stepped in front of Mr. Dimmick and fingered a bolt of white on white striped cotton. "What do you think, Mrs. Ward? How many yards do you think I'll need?"

As Pearl answered, Mr. Dimmick lifted his nose in the air, turned on his heel, and walked away.

"My heavens, what a stick in the mud. As if you can't have a conversation with a customer that's not about making a sale." Lillian huffed.

"He's serious about his job and that we present a very professional demeanor."

"What's wrong with developing rapport with the customers? We do it at the shop all the time. It builds loyalty. If people don't feel welcome, they don't come back. Doesn't he realize there are other dry goods stores in St. Joseph?"

"Did you really want the fabric? You don't have to purchase anything."

Lillian grinned. "Oh, I'm going to buy the fabric. I'd love a new dress. I think I'll take six yards. That will be enough to make the dress. Do you have any dressmaker patterns?"

"Yes, over here. We have McCall's and Butterick. There are several new styles. The skirts are being designed much narrower."

Pearl and Lillian looked through the patterns until they found one both liked. Once Pearl measured and cut the fabric, Lillian hugged her, paid for her purchase, and waved goodbye. As Pearl was putting the fabric bolt back in the rack she saw Lillian detour from a direct path to the exit to walk past Mr. Dimmick and 'accidentally' drop her bundle. Pearl turned away, smiling. Yes, Lillian was going to be a good friend.

Will saw the familiar hat through the window. He was sitting at his workbench, though he hadn't been getting much work done. Lillian had told him Pearl would be coming with more lace items today. He couldn't seem to keep his mind on the watch he was cleaning.

He stood, taking a towel and wiping his hands. The door opened, setting the attached bell jingling. Mrs. Ward entered carrying a parcel. She looked much better than when she'd come in last Saturday. There was color in her cheeks. The defeated air she'd had was gone. There seemed to be hope within her now.

"Good morning, Mrs. Ward. Lillian mentioned you'd be by with some more lace. Did she tell you we sold all you brought last week?"

"Yes, Mr. Miller, she did. Did she tell you she purchased dress goods?"

Will smiled. "Yes, she told me about your manager. Did you know she dropped her package right at his feet?"

"I did." She grinned back at him. "She thought he was very rude, I'm sure."

"That's my sister. She's about as subtle as a raging bull."

That made her laugh. It was a sweet laugh. One he could listen to all day.

"Mother isn't here at the moment. Father is feeling poorly and won't be in today. Mother stays with him most of the time."

"I'm sorry your father isn't feeling well."

"Thank you. She did say she would come sometime this morning. I hope you aren't in a hurry." Will hoped she had the time to wait.

"I'm not. I can stay a while. Would you like to see the lace? You could record them while we wait." She began to untie the string holding the parcel together.

While they were itemizing what Pearl had brought,

Lillian came down from the flat.

"Pearl, hello. Will, why didn't you let me know she was here? I would have come down sooner. Pearl, I have the dress all cut out. There's only one problem though. I forgot I was low on white thread. I'm going to have to go to a store and buy some more." Her eyes twinkled with mischief. "Do you think your boss would appreciate me going to another dry goods store rather than buy several spools at Townsend and Wyatt?"

Pearl chuckled. "If you drop them right at his feet, he just might."

"Oh, you saw that, did you? I just wanted to make sure he knew I was a paying customer."

"Thank you. As I'm a newly hired clerk, Mr. Dimmick seems to always be shadowing me. I'm sure he's only wanting to help me understand the job so I don't make mistakes."

"You are correct, I'm sure." Lillian's grin was wide and full of mischief.

"Would you want to help me inventory and tag each of these?" Will asked dryly.

"Of course, my dear brother. When is Mother arriving?"

They had just finished the recording when their mother entered the shop. "Good morning, my dears, Mrs. Ward. It's delightful to see you again. I see you brought more lace." She looked at her daughter. "Someone let you know all of yours sold."

"Yes," Pearl said. "Lillian was kind enough to come and tell me."

"And I helped Pearl keep her job. I'll have a new dress for the summer, too. As soon as I get it sewn, that is."

Will decided it was time to bring the topic back to the lace. His mother might make a comment about the number of garments his sister already had in her wardrobe. "Mother, you mentioned you wanted to speak with Mrs. Ward about specific items you would like her to create."

"Yes, thank you, Will." She turned to Pearl and explained what she'd like her to make.

~~~~~

Pearl counted her skeins of crochet thread. She would need to purchase more. There weren't enough with the same dye lot to make the sleeveless blouse. She didn't want there to be variations in the color of the thread even though the blouse would be made from white.

She had been surprised when Mrs. Miller asked her to make the garment. It was more complicated than the items she had taken to the shop both days. Rather than crochet the entire garment in one piece as she did most collars and handkerchief edging, she would have to make the motifs individually then crochet them together.

Pearl would take her thread and hook with her to work and crochet during her breaks and at lunchtime. If she was able to work on it consistently, the blouse could be done in two weeks.

Lillian was becoming a good friend. Saturday, Pearl and she had gone to the small park a few blocks away with a picnic lunch Lillian had packed.

They were only a little over a year different in age with Pearl being older. Lillian had moved in with her brother after her birthday in November last year.

"Mother and I were arguing all the time. Don't get me wrong. I love her, but she was driving me insane. She doesn't seem to realize I'm an adult. I want to manage my own life. Having to answer to her daily for every minute was absolutely awful.

"It was driving a wedge between us and between her and Father, too." Lillian flopped back on the grass, looking up at the puffy clouds floating in the blue sky. "He was the one who suggested I move in with Will. Mother wasn't happy, but I grabbed the opportunity." She chuckled. "I didn't even ask Will. I just packed and showed up at the shop with my luggage."

Pearl smiled. "I'll bet he was delighted. It's lonely living in an apartment by yourself."

"Oh, I'm so sorry. I didn't mean to remind you of your loss." Lillian turned on her stomach and, with contrite eyes, looked at Pearl.

"You didn't. I just know what it's like to live with someone other than your parents and now by myself." Pearl smiled at her friend. "So, was he delighted when you moved in?"

"No. His mouth dropped open when I announce he now had a roommate. He's a wonderful brother, though. He let me move in and hasn't complained. Much."

Pearl laughed. "He seems to be a caring man."

"He is. I don't know why he hasn't found someone to marry. Well, maybe I do. Mother can be rather intense when she wants to. Several years ago, Will brought a young lady home to meet the family. Mother was in one of her 'moods.' Few women can stand against her then." Lillian sat up and began packing the picnic basket.

Pearl had gone home after they went back. Lillian would work in the shop during the afternoon, allowing Will to concentrate on the repairs and orders for handcrafted brooches and pendants.

Pearl was sitting in the parlor of her flat by the window, taking advantage of the sunlight. She picked up her crochet hook and thread. She would practice the motifs for the blouse and make them into a collar. If it turned out well, she'd take it to the shop to sell. If she wasn't pleased with it, she could either wear it herself or pull it apart and use the thread for something else.

~~~~~

Will watched as his father entered the shop. He hated seeing this formerly vibrant man looking sickly and weak. Granted, his father was sixty-years-old, but until recently he'd enjoyed good health and vitality. Now, he was slightly stooped and moved much slower. He watched his steps rather than looking ahead.

"Good morning, Father. It's good to have you in the shop." Will walked around the counter in greeting.

"Yes, my boy. It is good to be back. Your mother, she's such a worrier. Where's the faith in God, I say?"

Will stepped aside to allow Matthew Miller to head to the workbench. "What are you working on today?"

"There were several watches brought in yesterday. I'm going to be cleaning them and making general repairs. Look at this one." Will handed a watch to Matthew.

"Well, it needs more than general repairs, I'd say."

The pocket watch was dented and the cover bent. It would take time, effort, and a great deal of care to make it work again.

"The owner said his three-year-old son got a hold of it and this is the result."

Matthew chuckled. "Little boys will do that. I remember when…"

Will sat and began working on the extremely damaged watch. His father reminisced about his son's childhood escapades, many of which Will had no recollection of. It wasn't quite like when he was learning the trade and they worked side by side, but it was good to have his father in the shop again.

"Where's your sister? Isn't she supposed to be here?"

"Lillian is making a delivery. Mother told you about the young woman making lace items for us to sell, didn't she?"

"Yes, a widow, correct?"

"Yes, Mrs. Ward. She does beautiful work. It's selling very well. She can hardly keep up with the demand. Her things are in that case." Will pointed, and Matthew stood slowly and walked to the display case.

Will spoke as he worked. "Mrs. Bacher, I believe you

know her. She's a friend of Mother's, the wife of Mr. Elmer Bacher who is president of the First National Bank. Mother had Mrs. Ward make a lace blouse for her, or her daughter, I can't remember the details. Anyway, Mrs. Ward brought it in Saturday. Lillian's delivering it."

"A lot of words centering around Mrs. Ward. She's a widow, you say?"

Will glanced at his father. He was grinning and had a twinkle in his eye that hadn't been seen a long while. "Yes, she lost him, let me think, about six weeks ago. Did Mother tell you about her situation?"

Matthew opened the display and picked up a lace collar. "Yes, such a sad story. Is she doing better now?"

"Yes, between her job at Townsend and Wyatt and the lace she's selling here, I believe she is able to pay her bills."

"Good. Do what you can to help her out, Will. Scripture says to aid the widows and orphans." The twinkle came in Matthew's eyes again as he looked at his son. "Is she pretty?"

Will glanced up from his work. He felt his face heat. "Yes, quite. She's becoming a good friend to Lillian."

"Ah." Matthew laid the lace down, straightening it.

The shop door opened admitting Lillian. "Father." She rushed over and hugged him. "I'm so glad to see you. How are you feeling?"

"Well enough."

She frowned. "Not a very high endorsement." Lillian opened the cash register and placed some bills in. "That Mrs. Bacher tried to get me to leave the blouse without paying for it. She said she didn't think she had enough in the house. That she would bring it in after she got it from her husband.

"She didn't fool me. I said she could pick it up when she brought the money in. Funny, she looked in her handbag and, low and behold, there was enough. Seems those with enough money don't always want to pay for their purchases, but if someone owes them... Bam. They are slapped silly for non-payment."

"Lillian," Matthew admonished. "Where do you learn these slang phrases?"

Will smiled and turned back to his task as his sister kissed their father's cheek in response.

CHAPTER FOUR

"Will," Lillian said after Pearl left the shop. "I think Pearl is lonely living by herself." She was dusting the jewelry in the display cases. Will was working on a commission piece. Lillian thought he was more talented than their father, and that was saying a lot.

"I'm sure it's a change. A sad change." Will didn't look up from his work.

"Yes, she said she's never lived alone before. She went from living at home with her parents to being married. They moved to St. Joe. Now, she's all alone in the city. She doesn't know very many people. They moved here in the fall. Winter didn't make it easy to meet people. Now, she's all alone." Lillian sighed.

Will set down his tool and looked at her. "You're up to something, little sis. What?"

Lillian turned around and looked at him. She grinned really big. "You know how you've been wanting to purchase a house, but you don't want to leave me here all alone? Well, I was thinking…" She paused for effect. Will just looked at her. "Pearl could move in here with me and you could buy your house and go live there."

"Am I that difficult to live with?"

"No, silly. But I do miss having another girl to talk with. Mary and Josey are busy with their children. Now with Josey being in an interesting condition again, she's even more unable to spend any time together."

"You really like Pearl, don't you?" Will stood and came over to her. He hugged her.

"Yes, I do. She's sweet and funny. And lonely. It would help her to move in here. The rent would be less expensive. Pearl's worried she won't be able to make the payments every month."

Will smiled. "Well, there is this house for sale on Clay Street I've been looking at. Maybe I'll see what the owner wants for it."

Lillian hugged him and gave him a big kiss on the cheek. "Thank you. You are the best brother."

"Don't thank me yet. I'm going to look at the house. There's no guarantee that I'll decide to buy it or they'll accept my offer."

"Sounds like I need to pray for both those things."

~~~~~

Will couldn't keep his eyes on his work and off Pearl as she and Lillian recorded the lace pieces she brought in. She was so pretty. Her skin was so creamy it seemed to glow.

Pearl was making larger items now: shawls, blouses, card table covers. They were selling well. They took longer to make but sold at a higher price. Will thought she had to be pleased with the additional income.

He knew Lillian was going to ask Pearl to move into the apartment with her. He'd purchased the house on Clay Street and was moving in slowly. He didn't have much furniture since he was leaving the apartment intact. He'd purchased a table and chairs last Tuesday. There wasn't much else he needed right away other than moving his bed and dresser. Will planned to take his time deciding on the pieces he wanted. Lillian had teased him about his bachelor quarters being only the bare necessities. She was right.

"Let's go upstairs and have some tea, shall we?" Lillian closed the ledger and patted the pile of lace sitting on the counter. "We can put these on display after we take a break." She looked at Will. "Do you want to come up?"

"Not at the moment. I'm nearly done with this watch. When I'm finished, I'll join you."

As Pearl passed by him, Will took note of her slim figure. Today, she was wearing a white dress made of similar fabric to the one Lillian had made. They seemed to be popular with the ladies during the summer. She wore a crocheted lace coat that he knew she'd made. That type of garment would be good as a commission piece.

He sniffed after she disappeared up the stairs. The faint aroma of gardenias lingered. It brought a smile to his face. Will blinked rapidly and shook his head. He needed to focus on his work, not dream about lovely young widows.

Will was placing the back cover onto the watch when he heard a squeal come from upstairs. Lillian must have asked Pearl to move in. Sounded like she was pleased with the notion.

He slipped the pocket watch into the paper wrapper with the customer's information on it and placed it in the completed order box. Going to the front, Will locked the door and placed the 'Back in 30 minutes' sign in the frame on the window. Now, he had some time to take a break with his two favorite ladies.

That thought stopped Will as he walked across the room. Since when was Pearl one of his favorite ladies? He'd known her less than a month. She was only coming to the shop on Saturdays. Lillian went to the dry goods store where Pearl worked at least once a week and brought back all sorts of news. Most was about Pearl, but his sister saw things and remembered conversations and people Will never even noticed.

That was it. He was mixing his affection for Lillian into his knowledge and liking for Pearl. He didn't know her all that well, after all. She was pretty, so that was contributing to his attraction.

With that thought, Will started walking again, confident he'd figured out why he waited anxiously for Saturday to come so he could see Pearl again.

~~~~~

As Pearl hugged Lillian, they both squealed with excitement. The huge weight of the rent payments was suddenly gone from her shoulders. Moving into the flat with her friend would make her life much easier. Townsend and Wyatt was only three blocks away. She could walk to work in just a few minutes rather than having to catch the electric trolley two blocks from where she lived and ride it across town. Being this close would save her lots of time. Time she could spend crocheting.

"Thank you so much, Lillian. You are an answer to prayer. I've been praying to find a less expensive place to live. All the ones I've looked at were simply awful. Rundown, dirty, no indoor plumbing, no electricity. They weren't that much cheaper than what I'm paying now."

"You'll only be paying half the rent now, since you'll be living with me."

Will stuck his head in the room from the enclosed staircase. "Is it safe to come in? I heard screaming."

"Oh, Will. You think you're so funny." Lillian waved a dismissive hand at her brother.

"I hear you are the proud owner of a new house, Mr. Miller," Pearl said. She sat on the davenport. Lillian went to the kitchen to get more tea. Will sat in the sewing chair.

"Yes, I've been thinking about buying a house. When Lillian mentioned she wanted a different roommate, I figured it was time."

"What? She said you wanted to buy a house and move out. She didn't want to be alone and asked if I wanted to come live with her." Suddenly the opportunity she thought was a gift from God dimmed.

"No, don't feel guilty. I'm explaining this poorly. I forget you don't know how Lillian and I tease each other.

I've been wanting to own a home, but I didn't want to leave Lillian here alone. I've been looking but hadn't pursued any purchase." He gave her a sly look. "When she mentioned she'd enjoy living with a strange female rather than her male relative, I figured now might be the best time to escape."

Pearl grinned. "I'm strange, am I?"

Will tipped his head, studying her. "Maybe not so strange, but then again, you just agreed to live with my sister. That's makes you suspect to being at least odd."

"I supposed that's true, Mr. Miller. However, since you are related to the one I will be living with, that might indicate you are a trifle odd yourself." She lifted her nose slightly and looked down it at him.

Will laughed. "Hoisted on my own petard. Since you will become more familiar, rather than strange, would you think it appropriate for us to be on a first name basis?"

This time it was Pearl who tipped her head in contemplation. "Yes, considering the circumstances, I do believe that would be appropriate, Will."

"Many thanks, Pearl."

"Will you two stop with the highfaluting attitudes. My heavens. It sounds like one of Mother's afternoon social teas with the ladies of the church."

Pearl and Will turned their heads without moving their shoulders and looked at Lillian. "We have determined that we are both strange since we associate with you," Will said. "That makes our behavior absolutely appropriate." He looked at Pearl, and they both started laughing.

~~~~~

"Why didn't you tell me about buying a house, Will? Did you mention it to your father?" Luella put her hands on her hips, staring down at him as he sat at the workbench.

Will focused on the brooch he was creating. It was a crescent with crystals in several shapes forming the design. He hadn't mentioned his purchasing the house to his mother because she would have taken over the process, not approving of any decision he made. He wasn't going to tell her that, however. The roof needed to stay on the building.

"I mentioned it to him. He thought it was a good idea. He said it was about time."

That flustered his mother. "Well, well, I do suppose so. You are twenty-two after all."

Will glanced up at her. "Mother, I'm twenty-four. Have been for several months now."

"Yes, Mother. He's more than three years older than I. I'll be twenty-one come November. Pearl is already. She'll be twenty-two in September."

"Enough talk about your ages. You're making me feel old."

Will and Lillian exchanged glances. Their mother always claimed her children were younger than they were. It was her way of denying her own age.

"So, when are you going to show me your new house, Will? After you move in or before?"

"How about after worship service tomorrow? I can hitch up the buggy and we can go after dinner. Fred and Clyde are coming with the wagon so we can move my bed and dresser. Those are the last of the furnishings I need to begin living there. Everyone in the family can see it at the same time that way. You were planning on all of us being home for Sunday dinner, weren't you?" Since that was the weekly routine, he knew the answer without her saying so.

"They knew about this house of yours, but I didn't?"

Will had realized his mistake the moment the words left his mouth. He'd hurt his mother's feelings. She was the last to know. "I'm sorry. I probably should have made sure you knew. It just happened so fast. Lillian made the suggestion. I looked at the house, made the offer, and suddenly I was the new owner. Then, I was trying to find time to look for some furniture and pack things and take them over, on the trolley."

Will could see his mother's attitude softening. She could bristle and become all prickly on the outside, but she was a softy inside. He remembered her concern for Pearl and her willingness to help the poor young widow.

"Lillian," he said. "Does Pearl have a telephone? We could move some of her things tomorrow since we'll have the wagon."

"No, she doesn't. She has a neighbor with one. I have the number. Shall I call and tell her we are coming tomorrow?"

"How about saying we will come for a while today. Then we can make plans for tomorrow. You and I could go over. Mother's here to mind the shop."

Lillian went to place the call.

"Oh, so you want me to do your work for you while you gallivant all over St. Joe?" Her twinkling eyes told him she wasn't offended by his presumption.

Will decided to tease her back just a little. He kissed her cheek. "Not my work, Mother. I'm the jeweler and watch repairman. You don't know how to do my job. All you need to do is to sell as much as you can of the merchandise in the shop."

"I'll do my best, dear." Luella patted him on the cheek and smiled.

~~~~~

The apartment building Pearl lived in wasn't rundown, but it was a bit shabby. Will was thankful that his sister suggested he buy the house so Pearl could move in with her. He wasn't confident a single young woman living alone here was safe.

"She said it was apartment 3-B." Lillian passed Will as he held the door open for her.

"She'll have one less flight of stairs to climb once she's

moved."

Pearl met them on the landing between the second and third floors. "I'm so glad you came but everything is at sixes and sevens. I'm trying to get things sorted and packed. I have to decide what to do with my furniture. There's not that much, but it won't fit in the apartment with all of yours."

Will and Lillian exchanged glances.

"We just might have a solution for you," Will said as they continued on to her apartment. He went on to explain the plans for the next day. "We could move you into the apartment after we move my bed and dresser."

"But what about my furniture? I don't know where to move it to."

Will smiled. "You can move it to my house. I can store it for you until you need it. I have the room."

Lillian snorted. "Several rooms with nothing in them. He's suggesting that he use your furniture to fill his house. That way he won't have to buy his own for a while. At least until you want it back."

Pearl looked at him, a wide grin on her face. "I think that is a perfect solution. It's a way I can pay you back for all the help you've given me."

"Oh no. I won't take it for nothing. I'll rent it from you. We'll reduce your rent of the apartment by the amount I'll pay to use your furniture."

"But…"

"No buts," Lillian said. She leaned close and whispered loudly, "Take him for as much as you can get. He can afford it. If all else fails, have him pay you in jewelry. He has plenty of it."

"Hey, sister of mine. You are supposed to be on my side, trying to get me the use of the furniture for as little as possible. Where's your familial loyalty?"

Lillian shrugged. "That went out the window many years ago when you put that dead snake in my bed."

Pearl laughed. "My brother did the same, but it was a dead frog."

"Brothers, first they do mean things to you, then they want your loyalty. Not the best plan." Lillian swept by Will and into the apartment. "Let's get as much ready as we can so we can move it tomorrow."

"I don't know what to do with these." Pearl indicated a pile of folded clothing on the kitchen table. It was men's clothing. "They were Patrick's."

"You could take them to a used clothing store. There are several in the city," Lillian suggested. "They'd buy them from you. They won't give you much for them."

"Or you could take them to one of the men's missions. Or the YMCA. They have men who need things." Will looked at the pile of garments, then back at Pearl. He didn't like to see the sadness in her eyes, but he understood the reason.

"I couldn't get rid of them before. It seemed so final, to give his things away. There wasn't a need to do so. They weren't taking up much space. Now that I'm moving, it's time. Still, it makes me sad." Pearl's eyes filled with tears. She looked from the table to Lillian and Will.

He wanted to pull her into his arms and comfort her. To hold her while she cried out her grief. But, it wasn't proper. Instead, he signaled Lillian with a subtle wave of his hand. She stepped up and did what he wanted to do.

~~~~~

Pearl joined the Miller family at their church the next morning. Lillian had insisted she worship with them and have Sunday dinner at her parents' house. That way, she said, Pearl could meet the rest of the strange family she was getting involved with.

They didn't seem strange or odd to her. They were a loving family who reminded Pearl of her own back in Ohio. The two older daughters were both married and had several children between them. The children ran and played and laughed. It took Pearl some time to figure out which child belonged to which set of parents.

Mary was the oldest and was married to Clyde Bethel. He worked as an accountant for the city. They had four children. Josephine, called Josey by her family, was married to Fredrick Gibson. He managed one of the many factories in town. Josey was expecting another child to add to their two.

Once the dinner dishes were washed and the younger children put down for naps, the men, along with Pearl, Lillian and Luella left to complete as much of the move as they could. Pearl had the apartment until the end of the month, so they planned to move the furniture today while they had the wagon. If they could complete that and move Will's few items, Pearl could get the rest of her belongings at her convenience. Lillian spoke up saying she would help with that so it would be accomplished more quickly.

~~~~~

"This is a cute house, Will," Luella said once she'd inspected every corner. "It's not that far from home either. That's convenient."

Will exchanged a look with his sister. They had commented to each other that its proximity was not one of its assets. Lillian simply shot him a wide toothed grin.

The house wasn't large. One story, the main rooms were two bedrooms, a parlor, and kitchen. The previous owner had divided the washroom so he could add a bathing room. There was indoor plumbing, and electricity had been wired when the remodel was done.

Pearl came into the parlor from the kitchen. "My small table works well in your washroom. I'm pleased you were able to find a place for all my furniture."

"I've contacted the telephone company to change the number. They will have done that by tomorrow if they haven't already. My number will be Juniper 3742."

Luella stepped to the window of the parlor. "Would

you like Lillian and me to make you draperies? I see there aren't any. You'll need them right away for your bedroom and the bathing room."

Will noticed Pearl blush at the mention of such personal rooms. "I'd appreciate that, Mother."

"Thank you for volunteering me," Lillian said, but she was smiling. Lillian loved to sew and would be very willing to make them. "Besides, it will give me a chance to go to Townsend and Wyatt to purchase the fabric."

Everyone laughed. Lillian loved to shop.

CHAPTER FIVE

"How do you like living in your own house, Will?" Matthew asked. He was examining several pieces of lace Pearl had left that morning for Lillian to record and display. He'd come to the shop after he and Luella had eaten lunch. He seldom came to work for a full day anymore. He just didn't have the stamina for the entire time. The journey on the trolley wasn't the joy it had been when it was first installed in the city.

Will set his tool on the bench and picked up a polishing cloth. "It's quiet. No Lillian talking all the time. I can actually hear myself think."

They both laughed. Lillian was known to be a chatterbox.

"You aren't lonely?"

"Not yet. It's been less than a week."

"Ah. I must say, your Pearl does fine lacework." Matthew laid the lace down, straightening it.

"She's not my Pearl. I think she may be Lillian's though. I stayed late last night working on this brooch. It needs to be ready by Friday. The laughter I heard coming from upstairs— Let's just say, they are enjoying living together."

Matthew moved to a case displaying cameo brooches and pendants. Opening it he took one out and held it up. "This one is especially lovely. It won't be here long."

The shop door opened admitting Lillian. "Father." She

rushed to the back and hugged him. "I'm so glad to see you. How are you feeling?"

"Well enough. Your mother fusses so. I'm not as young as I used to be, but I'm not a doddering old man just yet." Matthew set the cameo down, straightened it, and closed the display. He turned and walked toward his stool by the workbench. His legs suddenly wouldn't hold him and he collapsed while reaching out for the bench.

"Father!" Lillian cried.

Will was at his side in an instant. "Father, what happened?"

"Legs wouldn't support me. Went weak. Give me a moment. I'll be fine."

"Lillian," Will said. "Run down the block and around the corner. The Physicians & Surgeons Building is there. You'll be able to find a doctor there."

"No," Matthew protested. Lillian didn't pay attention. She ran out the door, in her hurry letting it slam shut.

~~~~~

Vernon Strasser carried his medical bag as he walked through the lobby of the Physicians' and Surgeons' Building. His office was on the top floor two flights up. He was headed out to make some house calls.

The door to the building banged open, startling him. A young woman ran in and up to him.

"Are you a doctor? I need one quickly," she asked, panic in her voice. She grabbed his hand and pulled him out of the building.

"What's the matter?"

"It's Father. He collapsed. Said his legs wouldn't support him. I don't think he can stand. Will's with him."

She was hurrying across the street, dragging him behind. A motorcar honked as they ran in front of it.

"How far?" Vernon asked.

"Just at the other end of the block. Bavarian Jewelry and Watch Repair Shop."

As they ran along the sidewalk, Vernon asked the young lady questions about her father. Name: Matthew Miller. Age: sixty. Known medical conditions. Those she was rather vague about. Her name: Lillian Miller. He briefly thought to inquire as to her age but decided now might not be the best time to ask that question.

The shop was on the corner and she opened the door and ran in before him. She scurried around the counter and dropped down out of sight. Vernon followed. On the floor lay a man with a younger man kneeling beside him.

"I'm Dr. Strasser. Can you tell me what happened?"

"He was standing at that display case. He turned around to come to the workbench and his legs went out from under him. I've made him stay lying here until you came." The young man stroked the older man's forehead.

"Can you tell me your name?" Vernon asked, taking in what he could of the symptoms Matthew exhibited. He was pale, a slight sheen of sweat covering his face.

"Matthew Miller." The words had a slight slur.

"Very good. That's what your daughter claimed it was. I'm glad she was correct." His small joke brought a slight grin to the right side of Matthew' face. "Look up at me, please." When he did, there was a droop to the left eyelid.

Taking hold of both hands, Vernon said. "Squeeze my hands, please, as tightly as you can." The right hand was much stronger than the left. He lay his patient's hands on his chest. He placed his hand on Matthew' left leg. "Press up." The leg pushed. It wasn't as strong as he'd hoped.

Vernon sat back on his heels. "You are exhibiting the symptoms of apoplexy. I think it is mild, but we'll need to do more testing to determine how badly you are affected."

Lillian gasped. "Oh, Father." She took hold of his hand.

"Now, Lillian, don't you fret. I'll be fine." Matthew squeezed her hand reassuringly.

"I'd like to have you transported to Elsworth Hospital.

There…" Vernon began, but Matthew cut him off.

"Just what are they going to do for me there?"

"Well, we can assess your symptoms and determine how much damage has been done."

"Are there assessments you can do there that you can't do at my home?"

"Well, no. From your ability to speak and move your arms and legs, it appears to have been a mild apoplexy." He went on to explain what had occurred and what the outcomes might be. Vernon glanced at Lillian. Tears were slipping down her cheeks.

"Since there's not much benefit to being in the hospital I'll just head home. If you want you can do further assessments there." His speech was improving. There wasn't as much slurring of the words.

"Father," the young man said. "If the doctor thinks you should be in the hospital, then you should listen to him." He turned his attention to Vernon. "I'm William Miller. Father and I run this shop together."

"Pleased to meet you, though not under these circumstances. Dr. Vernon Strasser." Vernon held out his hand, and Will shook it.

"Mother needs to be told," Lillian said.

"Yes, but don't call her on the telephone. That will only frighten her. You go fetch her, Will, and bring the buggy," Matthew said. "I'm not sure I can walk home, even riding the electric trolley most of the way." He began to roll over, seemingly intent on getting up. Vernon and Will helped him onto his desk chair.

Will stood looking at his father, then turned to Vernon. "Do you think he can get upstairs to the apartment?"

"Between us, I think we can get him there safely."

Although Matthew was weak, he was able, with Vernon and Will's support, to climb the stairs. They settled him on Lillian's bed while she fluttered around trying to help but also stay out of the way.

Will jumped off the trolley and hurried down the street. There were three blocks to traverse before he came to the house where he'd grown up.

How was he going to tell his mother what had happened? It was a question he'd thought about ever since he left the shop.

Dr. Vernon had left at the same time. He was going to return once he finished his house calls. He estimated it would take him approximately the same amount of time it would take to fetch his mother. Lillian would stay with their father. Will had locked the shop. Any customers would just have to come back another day.

He bounded up the front steps to the porch two at a time. Not bothering to knock, Will went into the house, calling for his mother. She came from the kitchen into the front hall wiping her hands on a towel.

"Will, what are you doing here?" It was evident she knew something was wrong.

"Mother, Father has had a spell. The doctor says it's an apoplexy. It was mild, and he's able to speak and walk, but he's weak. We need to take the buggy so we can bring him home."

Luella leaned against the wall.

"Mother, are you all right?" Will cupped her elbow in his hand.

"Just shocked. Give me a moment." She raised a shaky hand to her forehead and took a deep breath. She straightened and said, "How is he? What does he need? Let me get my hat. You go get the horse hitched. I'll be out in a jiffy." She headed for the stairs pulling her apron ties as she went. "Wait. No, go. I can't think." She covered her face with her hands.

Will placed an arm around his mother and gave her a hug. "His speech is a little slurred and his left side is weaker than the right. The doctor said it was a mild episode. Lillian is with him. He's resting in the apartment. He wouldn't go to the hospital. He just wants to be home with you."

"He said that?"

"Maybe not in so many words, but yes."

Luella chuckled. "No, he wouldn't say so." She patted Will on the cheek. "Go get the buggy ready. I'll meet you out front."

By the time Will drove around the house, Luella had changed from her work dress to a walking dress, was wearing her spring hat, and was standing on the sidewalk. Will secured the reins and began to get down to help her, but she was already climbing into the buggy.

"Let's go. No time to waste."

On the drive through town, Will explained more fully what had happened and what Dr. Strasser had said. His mother listened, asking a question occasionally. Then, silence fell between them.

Will halted the horse on the less traveled street by the shop which was on the corner, jumped down and tied him to the electric pole. He helped Luella down, and followed her into the shop after he unlocked the door. They hurried over to and up the stairs. Lillian met them at the top. The women hugged.

"He's sleeping. Dr. Strasser hasn't returned. He hasn't telephoned either. He said he would before he returned. I gave him our number."

Luella laid her gloves on the table and placed her hat beside them. "I'm going to go see him. Please give me a moment before you come in."

Will and Lillian waited while their mother went into the bedroom.

~~~~~

"Plaza 8585, please," Dr. Strasser told the operator. He was finished with his house calls and was using his patient's telephone to contact the Millers. The number rang several times before it was answered.

"Hello? Bavarian Jewelry and Watch Repair Shop." The voice was Lillian's. Vernon knew he should think of her as Miss Miller but didn't want to.

"This is Dr. Strasser. I've finished with my calls and will be coming to check on your father now. How is he doing?"

"He's sleeping. Mother is here and with him."

"Good. I'll grab the trolley and be there as soon as I can."

"Thank you."

Vernon left the house and hurried to the trolley stop. When he arrived at the shop, Lillian was waiting at the door. Letting him in, she locked it and they hurried upstairs. The sway of her hips as she preceded him caught his eye. He pushed the thought away.

Vernon was used to seeing worry and concern on people's faces. It was part of the stressful profession he'd chosen. Lillian's expression made more of an impact on him though. She seemed so vulnerable. So afraid she would lose her father. It made him want to wrap his arms around her and give her what comfort he could. That wouldn't be appropriate behavior for either a doctor or a single man to a single woman, of course. Especially one he'd only met a few hours before.

Rather than wake his patient, Vernon had the rest of the family move to the parlor where he explained what had happened and what to expect in the days to come. "He'll need to rest. His body has gone through a shock and needs to recuperate. I'll come by every couple of days to check on his progress. In about a week, he'll have an exercise regimen to do daily. It will help him regain his strength."

Vernon pulled out his pocket watch. "It's late enough in the day, I can stay until he wakes and help him down the stairs." He didn't want to leave. There was a young lady who piqued his interest.

"I'd be most appreciative, Dr. Strasser," Mrs. Miller said. "My sons-in-law are still at work. Having another strong man along with Will to help my husband down the stairs takes a worry off my mind."

They sat in the parlor wanting to give Mr. Miller as much rest as they could before moving him to his home. Lillian made tea and served it with a plate of cookies. Vernon couldn't keep his eyes off her. She was cute and perky and talked a lot.

The bell attached to the front door of the shop jingled. Will stood. "That will be Pearl. She lives with Lillian."

Another pretty woman came in. She didn't look like any of the Miller family.

"Oh, hello. I didn't expect to see so many up here," she said.

"Mrs. Ward, this is Dr. Strasser. Father suffered an apoplexy seizure. He's in Lillian's room sleeping." Will moved across the room and laid a hand on her arm.

"Oh, I'm so sorry. Will he be all right?"

Vernon watched as Will explained. He wondered why Mrs. Ward was living with Lillian.

"Is there anything I can do to help?" she asked. Mrs. Miller assured her that they would let her know if there was a way for her to.

"Luella." Mr. Miller's call brought them all to their feet. His wife hurried into the bedroom. Vernon followed Will and Lillian.

Soon, they were helping him down the stairs and into the buggy. Will drove his parents home, leaving Vernon with Lillian and Mrs. Ward standing on the sidewalk watching the buggy depart.

CHAPTER SIX

Pearl crossed her arms over the calendar lying on the table and dropped her head to rest on them. What was she going to do? Just when things began to look up, now this. Being offered the opportunity to live with Lillian had been a Godsend. It had lowered her expenses dramatically.

But now— now she was going to lose her job. There was no way she could support herself on what she could make crocheting lace. Not herself and a baby.

When she missed her first course, Pearl had thought it was due to the stress of Patrick's death. There was no reason other than one to have missed the second. She must have conceived just before Patrick became sick.

At least she now knew why she was so tired. Pearl was grateful she wasn't suffering from morning sickness and hoped that blessing would continue. She didn't know what she would do if she started becoming ill at work, or so she couldn't go to work.

Living only three blocks from the dry goods store now was a blessing for several reasons. It meant she didn't have to ride the trolley both ways. That saved her money. Money she needed to save for the baby. The time she saved not having to wait for the trolley and ride it definitely was beneficial. It gave her nearly an hour more of sleep in the morning.

Pearl had hoped to fill the time crocheting both before and after work. Her fatigue took over though, making it impossible to stay awake after she returned to the apartment in the evening.

Pearl couldn't decide whether she was happy to be having Patrick's child or not. Having a part of him live on brought joy, but knowing she would be out of work as soon as she began to show was distressing. She thought she was about two months along. If she was fortunate, she might be able to keep her condition secret for three more months at the longest.

It was Saturday, so she wasn't working at the dry goods store. That meant she could spend the day crocheting. Larger items like shawls and tablecloths made the most money, but they also took the longest to make. Gloves sold well also, especially with June weddings coming. She'd already sold several pairs.

Pearl put the calendar away and got her basket containing her thread and hooks. Not wanting to be upstairs alone, she headed down to the shop. Lillian would be there, as would Will. Maybe they would allow her to sit out of the way and do her crocheting there.

Will looked up and smiled when she came down the stairs. "Good morning. We were hoping you would join us. No sense in you hiding away when we can keep each other company."

Pearl smiled. "Thank you, I was hoping for that very thing." She sat on Matthew's desk chair and took out her hook and thread, beginning on a pair of gloves.

"How do you enjoy living with my sister? Or shouldn't I ask so you don't have to answer that question? It might be awkward if you hate it." Will chuckled.

"I'm liking it very much. Lillian is fun and easy to be with. Of course, it's only been a week. Maybe in another week it will be awful," Pearl teased. "How is your father? Lillian hasn't said much."

"Weak, but doing better. He's not the best patient. Mother has come to the shop several times, just to get away from the growly bear, as she says. Lillian went to visit, so I anticipate Mother coming in for a while."

Pearl nodded. "I was wondering where she was."

A customer came in then, so Will went to tend to him. Pearl crocheted, listening to the conversation. The bell on the door jingled, and Mrs. Miller walked in. She came straight to the back.

"Pearl, good morning. Lillian mentioned how pleased she is to have you living with her."

"I'm enjoying the change in living accommodations as well. This apartment is much nicer than my previous one."

Luella preened at the compliment. "Thank you."

"How is Mr. Miller fairing?"

Luella's shoulders slumped slightly. "He seems to be getting stronger. It's slow. Definitely slower than he'd like."

The shop door opened and closed causing both ladies to look toward the front. Will stepped away from the cash register with a smile. "A very profitable way to start the day. I just sold an engagement and wedding ring. He also bought a pair of gloves for his fiancé"

"Congratulations." Pearl dropped her eyes when Will's focus centered on her.

"That's wonderful," Luella said. "That brings me to the topic I want to speak to you about, Pearl. Mrs. Bacher, the woman who purchased the sleeveless blouse; she wants a black shawl made. It's to be of black silk thread. Also, she would like to meet you and discuss the design. Would you be able to go and meet her?"

Pearl hesitated. "If that's what she wants, I suppose so."

"I'll go with you, but mustn't stay for the entire discussion. Matthew will need me. Is now convenient?"

"Well, yes."

"Good, I'll call her and make arrangements." Luella went to the back wall where the telephone was mounted and cranked the handle.

"Are you uncomfortable with going?" Will asked.

Pearl noted the concern in his eyes. "A little. I don't know the woman. I'm not sure how to proceed."

"Just follow Mother's lead. She's familiar with Mrs. Bacher. All you need to do is be your charming self."

Luella finished her telephone call and came back to where Pearl and Will were seated by the workbench. "Good news. Mrs. Bacher is coming downtown and would like to meet us at the Tea Room. She's planning on going shopping at Townsend and Wyatt. She will be there in a half an hour."

Pearl stood, wavering just a moment when her head swam.

"Are you all right?" Will asked, reaching his hand out to support her arm.

"Yes, I just got up too quickly. I think it's the excitement of a large order and going to the Tea Room."

~~~~~

Will looked up when the door to the shop opened, setting the bell jingling. Pearl entered with a huge smile on her face. She ran around the counter, excitement radiating throughout her entire being. She looked so pretty in her pale blue tea dress with its puff sleeves and pink Irish lace on the yoke. Will thought it was a very smart way of highlighting how proficient Pearl was at making lace.

"You won't believe this, Will. Mrs. Bacher wants me to make her a large shawl. She gave me the money to purchase the black silk thread. I'll be able to get it at a discount because I work at Townsend & Wyatt. Your mother was very helpful. She suggested the price the shawl should be, and Mrs. Bacher agreed. She left to go home when we began discussing the designs."

"That's wonderful. How long do you think it will take you to complete?" Will asked.

Pearl's eyes were shining with elation, making her even

more beautiful. "Several weeks. That is, if I can work on it steadily. I need to figure the amount of thread I'll need. Then, I'm going to Townsend and see if they have enough of the same dye lot. If not, I'll place an order. I hope they have it so I can start today. I made sure all the motifs were simple ones for the design. That was your mother's idea, also. She's right. There's no sense in making it more complicated than it needs to be. The general public doesn't know a simple motif from an intricate one."

Will grinned. Pearl was sounding like Lillian when she got excited about something. He liked seeing joy in her eyes. Too often Pearl's grief showed. Maybe she was simply tired from the move, her job, and making so many lace items. Nearly every day she left a piece or two on the counter as she left to go to work. He'd find them, record them in the ledger and display them in the case. The shop's reputation for having high-quality Irish lace was growing in large part because of the items she made.

"Do you want some paper to figure on? I have some scratch paper here." Will opened a drawer and took out several sheets of paper with writing on one side. He laid them, blank side up and placed a pencil on them beside his workspace.

He'd done some rearranging of his work area during the past week. Lillian had been nagging him to clean the bench so she'd have more space to do the bookwork. That hadn't been the motivation for him to get it done though. Will hoped Pearl would find the spot welcoming to spend her time crocheting there instead of up in the apartment.

Yesterday, Will had stayed later than normal claiming he had work to complete. Lillian had gone upstairs to fix supper, and he'd been invited to stay for it. Pearl had sat next to him making a lace antimacassar set. It now was prominently displayed in the case. Will expected it to be sold within a few days.

He'd enjoyed their time chatting as they both did their

work. Maybe he'd do some rearranging of the entire space. The desk chair, used first by his father and now mostly by Lillian, couldn't be the most comfortable for Pearl to sit in to crochet. Maybe he'd look into getting a sewing chair similar to the one in the apartment. That would be much more welcoming. It would also give Pearl somewhere to sit if Lillian was here.

"Well, I'm off. I've got the necessary yardage figured for the thread. If I hurry to Townsend now and I can get what I need, I should be able to start on the motifs and get several made today."

Will watched Pearl leave. The more he saw of her, the more he liked her. The day she'd fainted in his shop had become one of the best days of his life.

CHAPTER SEVEN

"Pearl, Pearl. Are you all right? Wake up." Lillian shook her friend by the shoulder. She hadn't realized Pearl hadn't gotten up that morning. She was due at the dry goods store in a half an hour.

"What?" Pearl rolled to her back.

"You need to get up or you'll be late for work. You only have thirty minutes."

"What?" Pearl shrieked. She threw back the covers and jumped out.

Lillian watched as Pearl grabbed the clothing she needed. "Here, let me help." Between the two of them, they soon had Pearl dressed. While she brushed her teeth and washed her face, Lillian arranged her hair in a simple style acceptable to Townsend & Wyatt's dress code.

"Here." Lillian handed Pearl her handbag and a piece of buttered bread when she straightened from buttoning her shoes. "Eat this on the way. I'll come by later with some lunch for you. Now, go."

Pearl flew down the stairs as Lillian watched. Something was wrong with her friend. This was the first time she had overslept, but she was always tired. They'd sit in the parlor after supper and chat while Pearl crocheted and Lillian sewed. Every evening she fell asleep within a few minutes. The shawl for Mrs. Bacher wasn't progressing very quickly.

Lillian picked up the bag Pearl kept her motifs, hook,

and thread in. Normally, she took it with her and crocheted during her breaks and her lunch hour. She'd forgotten to take it in her hurry to get to work on time. Lillian would deliver it when she took food for Pearl later this morning.

Lillian made Pearl's bed and put away the nightgown she'd left on the floor. Pearl was definitely neater than Lillian. Her room had things lying on just about every surface. Everything of Pearl's was put away. The contrast made Lillian smile.

Heading down to the shop, she found Will just arriving. She debated mentioning Pearl oversleeping but decided her friend might not appreciate something so personal being discussed with a man. She would tell him about Pearl not taking her lunch to work since Lillian would need to leave the shop to take it.

"Good morning, little sis," Will said. "Beautiful June day, isn't it?"

"Yes," Lillian said.

"I saw Pearl nearly running down the street. Was she late heading for work?"

"Yes, the morning just got away from her. She even forgot her lunch. I'll take it to her later, when I go to visit Father."

~~~~~

"I saw you rushing up the street, Mrs. Ward," Mr. Dimmick said when Pearl came from the Lady's Employee Lounge. It wasn't a lounge in the truest sense of the word, rather a room for the female employees to place their coats, bags, and any other of their belongings while they worked. It was also where they took their breaks and ate their lunches.

"Yes, I didn't want to be late. Time was a bit short this morning." Pearl nearly reached up to look at the watch-locket she'd always worn pinned to her bodice. She stopped her hand just in time, her heart sinking. There was no way she'd be able to buy the locket back. Not with the expenses coming and her losing her job.

"Commendable, but a flushed and perspiring employee isn't a welcoming presence for the customers."

"No, sir." Pearl couldn't tell if that was the correct response or if Mr. Dimmick wanted a 'yes, sir' instead. He simply turned on his heel and walked away. "What a grouch," Pearl mumbled as she went to the fabric department where she worked.

There was a shipment of new fabrics waiting to be placed in the racks. The ends needed to be labeled with the price per yard. As she did so, Pearl noticed a fabric she thought Will might like for the draperies in his parlor. Lillian and Mrs. Miller had completed the ones for his bedroom and the bathing room.

Just a few days earlier they had come and purchased cotton to use in the kitchen and washroom. Pearl thought lace ones would have been pretty in the kitchen but hadn't suggested it. That left the parlor and the second bedroom still needing window coverings. This fabric was good quality and well suited for draperies in a parlor. She would show it to Lillian when she came with Pearl's lunch.

It was a busy morning and Pearl was surprised when Lillian showed up. She looked at the clock above the elevator and saw it was nearly her lunch break. When she'd had her morning break a couple of hours earlier, she'd realized her crocheting had been left behind and mourned the loss of the few minutes she could have worked on motifs for the shawl. They were nearly completed and she would begin connecting them as soon as they all were.

The shawl was taking longer than Pearl had hoped due to her fatigue. Falling asleep in the evenings shortened the time she could work on it, and she'd made more mistakes and had to rip out the work and correct the stitches. That took time. Time Pearl didn't want to lose. Couldn't afford to lose.

"Hello, sleepyhead," Lillian whispered as she gave Pearl a quick hug. "I've brought you lunch and your crocheting."

"Oh, you're a doll. Thank you." Pearl placed the bags under the counter. "My break is in about ten minutes. Would you like to stay and eat with me? There's a bench outside that's in the shade."

Lillian grinned and help up her handbag. "I brought my lunch hoping you'd want me to."

Pearl showed the drapery fabric to Lillian, who bought a small piece to show Will and her mother. "I don't want to choose something he won't like and Mother won't have input for. That's a mistake I made with the bathing room. She was not happy not being included in the decision. I learned my lesson. I sort of pity the woman Will marries. It will be difficult for Mother to relinquish the control of his life she still has. He'll need to set her straight about who is the most important woman in his life. Leave and cleave, the Bible says."

"That was one of the reasons Patrick and I moved from Ohio." They were sitting on the bench enjoying the fresh air as they ate. "Both our mothers were constantly meddling in our lives. They both thought we needed advice. It was causing conflict between him and me. Loyalty to our parent and resenting the input of the other. When we realized we hadn't set the other as the most important person in our lives, we adjusted our perspective. It didn't make our mothers very happy. We finally had to move away."

"That's sad. I hope that doesn't happen to Will or me. Mary and Josey are both able to sort of ignore Mother when she gets into her moods. It's harder for me since I'm the baby of the family. Will is the only boy. He'll inherit the shop.

"It's gone to the first boy in every generation since Wilhelm Mueller came to America from Bavaria in 1850. I think it goes even further back. Wilhelm wasn't the first son. He got out of Bavaria before he could be drafted and have to fight in the battles that led to the Agreement of Olmütz. It has something to do with uniting Germany or something like that. Anyway, it's why Wilhelm immigrated to America." Lillian took a bite of her sandwich.

"Is Will named after your ancestor?"

"Yes, my grandfather Wilhelm married on the way over to Bridget Ryan from Ireland. Father changed the spelling from Mueller to Miller when he came of age."

Pearl took out her crocheting as soon as she finished her meal. By the time her half hour break was over she'd completed another of the motifs.

"You do that so quickly. That hook just flies," Lillian said.

"I've been crocheting since I was seven. My grandmother lived with us. My grandfather died in the Civil War. She never remarried, and she and her children lived with her parents until my mother married my father. She lived with us then. She and my mother taught me to crochet. 'Idle hands are the devil's workshop.' That was my grandmother's motto.

"We'll need to finish this discussion tonight. I need to get back to work."

They stood and Lillian took the remains of the meal with her. Pearl went back to work under the watchful eyes of Mr. Dimmick.

~~~~~

Lillian watched Pearl as they fixed supper. Her eyes had dark shadows under them. Her shoulders drooped. Something was definitely wrong, and she intended to find out what it was. She wasn't her mother's daughter for nothing. Determination was practically her middle name.

Only she and Pearl sat down to eat. Will was dining

with their parents tonight. It seemed that he stayed late at the shop several times a week, joining them for the evening meal. Lillian knew he didn't like to cook and barely knew how. She also wondered if Pearl was a draw.

Will had rearranged the back part of the shop, even moving the counter and several display cases forward to make more room. He'd brought an old sewing chair from home and set it at the end of the workbench. His end of the workbench. It was for Pearl to sit in when she was there on Saturdays. Lillian could sit in the chair during the week, but it seemed to be reserved for Pearl on the weekend.

"You go on to the parlor. I'll just wipe the table and be in momentarily," Lillian said. As she ran the dishcloth over the table, she watched Pearl walk into the other room, pick up her crocheting, and sit down. Rather than take her work from the bag, Pearl just sat, staring off into space. With determination, Lillian finished her task. She was going to get to the bottom of what was wrong with her friend.

Rather than settling into the sewing chair, Lillian sat next to Pearl on the davenport. Taking her friend's hand, she looked at the pale weary face. "Pearl, what's wrong? No, don't deny it. I can tell something is. You come home from work exhausted. You fall asleep early in the evening, sitting here while we chat and do our handwork. This morning you overslept, nearly to the point of being late for work. I had to wake you up. I'm so worried. Are you ill?"

She watched as tears gathered in Pearl's eyes. Her heart clenched. Pearl had become more than a close friend over the past few weeks. Lillian was beginning to love her like a sister.

She gathered Pearl into her arms. "What is it? Whatever it is, I'll help anyway I can. I know Will would, too."

Pearl drew back. "Oh, you mustn't tell him. No,

please."

"Sweetheart, unless I know what's going on I can't promise anything."

Pearl gave a small bitter laugh. "Patrick gave me something before he got sick. It's something we wanted so much. Then he died. Now, I don't know whether to be happy or sad. Thankful or terrified. I bounce between the emotions so many times each day. It's going to be so difficult, but God will provide. He did with you wanting me to live here. Maybe I'll be able to support myself only on the crocheting, but I don't know. There's just so much uncertainty. I'm just so tired all the time, it's hard to think."

"I don't understand. You'll have to be more specific. What is the matter? Are you ill?"

"No, not ill. I'm expecting."

Lillian stared at her friend. Relief followed by joy swamped her. What a blessing. No wonder Pearl was so tired, after working all day on her feet. Then, Lillian realized why Pearl was concerned. "You're afraid you are going to lose your job."

"I'm certain I will lose my job. As soon as it becomes obvious that I'm in the family way, I will be let go. Then, how am I going to support myself and the baby? Even after it is born, I can't be gone all day working. Who will take care of it? Where are we going to live? How will I make enough money making lace to feed, clothe, and afford a place to live?"

Tears slid down Pearl's face. Lillian hugged her again. She didn't know what to say or how to fix the situation.

"Please, Lillian, please, don't tell anyone. At least not yet. It will come out soon enough. I need time to figure out what I'm going to do. If Mr. Dimmick finds out, I'll be fired. I need the job for as long as I can hold it."

Lillian released the hug and patted Pearl's hand. "I won't say a word. We'll find a solution. You know you can stay here with me for as long as you want."

"Thank you. You're a dear friend, and I love you."

"I love you, too. Now, you have a shawl to finish that will earn you a very good commission to finish, and I have these curtains to hem. Before we get busy with those, we are going to take your situation to the only One who knows how it will end."

The two women joined hands, bowed their heads, and began to pray.

CHAPTER EIGHT

Will climbed the stairs to the apartment. It was Saturday and Pearl was preparing lunch. Lillian was visiting their parents. Their father was getting stronger, but Will doubted if he would ever come back to work in the shop. It saddened him to think the few years they'd had to work side by side were over.

Pearl had spent the morning sitting in the sewing chair he'd placed at the end of the workbench, working on the shawl she was making for Mrs. Bacher. After she'd gone upstairs Mrs. Douglas Clary, wife of the president of the electric company, came in and asked about the young woman who made such beautiful lace. Her daughter was getting married and Mrs. Clary wanted to speak with Pearl.

"It's not quite ready, Will. It will be about fifteen more minutes," Pearl said when he entered the kitchen.

"Are you making something that can be held for a while?"

"Yes, it's soup and sandwiches. Why?"

"A woman came in and would like to see you. She has a commission she'd like to speak with you about. It's Mrs. Clary." Will explained who she was while Pearl washed her hands and took off her apron.

"Is my hair in place? I don't want to keep her waiting but don't want to appear slovenly either."

Will gave a twisted grin and captured a thin lock of her

blonde hair that had escaped, tucking it back into place. "You look fine. Come, she's waiting." He reached for her hand but stopped himself. Instead he stepped back, allowing her to precede him down the stairs.

He listened from his seat at the workbench while Mrs. Clary and Pearl discussed what she wanted made. It would be a coup for Pearl if she was allowed to make the lace gown to top the silk underdress for the woman's daughter. The Clarys were even more influential than the Bachers in St. Joseph society.

"I'll be able to meet with you on the twenty-fifth. I have another commission I should finish this week and need to deliver next Saturday. I can work up some motif designs to bring with me when I come."

"Very good. I'm sure they will be lovely. I must leave now. So many details to consider for the wedding. Please call before you come on the twenty-fifth. I want to be sure we are both there, Daisy and I."

"Yes, Ma'am. I will."

Will watched as Pearl stood stock still as Mrs. Clary left the shop. Then, she spun in a circle to face him.

"Can you believe it? Can you? I can't. An entire dress. For a wedding. Her daughter's wedding. The amount of commission will be phenomenal. Yes, it will be a lot of work, but the people who see it will know I made it. Surely, it will bring more custom work." Pearl was bouncing with excitement. Joy was written all over her being.

Will stood, his smile was wide. "I'm pleased for you."

Pearl bounced over to him and gave him a big hug. "Thank you so much for everything you've done for me." She released him and dashed to the stairs. "I'm so excited. I can't wait to tell Lillian. She'll be delighted. I'll go up and set lunch out on the table. You must be starving. I know I am. Oh, I'm so happy."

Will chuckled as she dashed up the stairs. Seldom had he seen her so happy. Lately, there seemed to be an anxiety hovering over her. Almost a desperation. Never did she complain or express any worry. Pearl was always polite and often showed wit and charm in her conversation.

As he thought about the past few weeks, Will realized she'd become more quiet. She concentrated her attention more on her crocheting than visiting. She also looked tired.

Many evenings Will stayed for supper with his sister and Pearl. She came home shortly after Will closed the shop. Townsend and Wyatt closed at the same time. He'd noticed her fatigue and even mentioned it a few times. If he commented on it, Pearl just said it had been a long busy day.

After supper they would chat in the parlor while Lillian washed the dishes. That was a change. They had done them together when Pearl first moved in. Now, Lillian insisted that Pearl go sit and crochet while she did the work. His sister said it was so he didn't have to be by himself in the parlor. That had never bothered her while he lived there.

Will walked over and locked the door, placing the 'Back in 30 minutes' sign in the window. He'd talk with Lillian about his concerns early next week while Pearl was at work.

~~~~~

"I have a few things to take care of up here," Pearl said after they ate their lunch. "It may take an hour or so. Then I'll come down and do my crocheting in the shop. I want to get this shawl done so I can begin working up the design for the wedding dress."

She and Will were doing the dishes. He had insisted on helping. There wasn't much to do. They didn't eat dinner at noon but had a lighter lunch. Supper in the evening was their main meal of the day. Lillian would be home to fix it.

"Okay, you know I'll miss you. I look forward to our visits." Will took the plate from her hand and began drying it.

In truth, Pearl was going to take a nap. She wasn't going to tell Will that, however. She was exhausted.

As excited as she was about the new commission, Pearl was concerned about getting it made in time. If her fatigue continued she was afraid she'd make mistakes and have to tear out the stitches, redoing the work.

Will went down to open the shop. Pearl wiped the last of the crumbs from the table and went into her bedroom. She'd lie down for an hour. Then she would go down and spend the rest of the afternoon in the shop. Lillian would be back by then. Pearl fell asleep designing the wedding dress in her head.

"Pearl, Pearl. Are you all right?" Lillian's concerned voice woke Pearl.

"Yes, why?" She opened her eyes and stretched.

"It's almost three o'clock. Will's getting concerned."

"Three? Oh, I never intended to sleep this long. Nearly three hours." Pearl threw the coverlet she'd used off and sat up. Her head spun with her quick movement. She placed a hand to her forehead.

"Are you sure you are okay?" Lillian laid a hand on her shoulder.

"I sat up too quickly. I feel fine now. I'll get my crocheting. I need something to tell Will that won't make him suspicious of anything. I don't want anyone else to know of my condition yet."

"I understand. Why not just say you were tired from a busy week, laid down for a while and just woke up? The truth is always best. You don't have to say anything else. After all, Scripture says in Proverbs 12:23 that a wise man doesn't reveal all he knows."

Pearl chuckled as they headed down the stairs. "Can't argue against the Word."

Will studied her with worried eyes. Before he could say anything, Pearl spoke. "I'm sorry. Lillian said you were concerned." She went on with the truth, as her friend had suggested, just leaving out the small detail of what was causing her extreme fatigue.

The concern on Will's face faded. "So, are you rested now?"

"Yes, and ready to get as much done on this shawl as I can today. It's to be delivered next Saturday."

~~~~~

"Mrs. Ward, will you please come to my office?" Mr. Dimmick said. His ever present frown accompanied the words.

Pearl had just finished waiting on a customer and was placing the bolt of fabric back in its place. "Of course, Mr. Dimmick."

Pearl's heart raced. Did he know of her condition? Was she going to be fired? Her clothing wasn't getting tight yet. There wasn't a way he could know. Could he? The only person who knew was Lillian. She'd never break the confidence, especially to Mr. Dimmick. Whenever Lillian came to shop, she made sure to walk past the man with the parcel containing what she'd purchased.

"Please close the door," he instructed when they were both in the small room.

Pearl was uncomfortable with the notion so she left it cracked open.

"I've noticed you have been crocheting quite a lot during your breaks."

"Yes, sir. I make lace to sell in the Bavarian Jewelry and Watch Repair Shop."

"When I noticed your activity, I had thought I might need to warn you not to be doing so during working hours, but you've never done so."

"No, sir. I would never do so. I'm paid to work at Townsend and Wyatt, not do my other work even if the day is slow."

"Commendable. Some employees don't seem to understand that concept." Mr. Dimmick paused. "Mrs. Ward, my wife is a semi-invalid. She isn't able to get out much. I was wondering if you could make a lace bed-jacket for her? We can't really discuss it now. I don't want to be an employee who abuses my employer's trust. May we meet after work to discuss the project?"

"Yes, sir. If it would be acceptable to you, could we meet at the shop? I live above it with the owner's sister. It's only a few blocks away."

"That would be fine. I know the shop. This evening?"

"Yes, sir."

Mr. Dimmick actually smiled. "Thank you. Now, for the other reason I've called you here. You've been working here long enough now that you will receive an increase in your hourly wage. It's a way Townsend and Wyatt uses to encourage their employees to stay on."

Pearl just barely kept her jaw from falling open. She'd never expected a raise. It wasn't a huge amount but every little bit helped. Plus he was offering her commission work. Maybe he wasn't such a sour puss, as Lillian called him, after all.

Pearl thought about her crochet work. If she continued to get larger commissions, maybe she would be able to support herself after she lost her job and the baby came. It wouldn't be stable and consistent work. She would have to be very frugal. Pearl was saving every extra penny knowing money was going to become tighter very soon. She had, at most two more months before her time at Townsend and Wyatt came to a close.

~~~~~

Will watched Pearl enter the shop. He'd expected her to be beaming with excitement. She had been earlier in the week when she'd rushed home from work saying she had a client coming to meet with her in a short while. When she told them who it was, Lillian dropped the tray of cameos she was holding. Fortunately, none broke.

"He what?" Lillian had squealed.

"Mr. Dimmick wants me to make a bed-jacket for his wife. She's a semi-invalid. He wants to give her a gift she can enjoy, he said. He'll be here in just a few minutes. I'm going to run upstairs and wash and straighten my hair. If he gets here, keep him entertained until I get back, please."

"Will do," Will said to her back as she ran up the stairs.

The rest of the week Pearl had been happy. She'd been grieving when they met. Then she'd seemed to start enjoying life after her loss. Especially after she moved in with Lillian. His sister brought joy to everyone just by being herself.

Lately, Pearl's mood had been slipping back into despondency. There was an anxiety within her. She never said anything, just went about her business, but the tenor of her spirit seemed to have almost a desperation to it.

This morning, Pearl had left to deliver the shawl to Mrs. Bacher. She'd been so happy. The shawl was a large beautiful triangle in deep black silk. Long fringe framed the two shorter sides. Floral and foliage motifs were artfully arranged and connected with scrolls and chain stitches.

Now, Pearl entered the shop nearly in tears. She wasn't carrying the package she'd left with so the shawl must have been delivered. He hurried to meet her, needing to know what was wrong.

"Pearl, what's the matter? Didn't Mrs. Bacher like the shawl?"

Tears slipped down Pearl's cheeks. "She loved the shawl. She thought it was beautiful. She's wearing it to the theater tonight."

Will ran his finger gently across her cheek wiping the moisture away. "Then why?"

"She only paid me a quarter of what we agreed upon.

She said that's all the money she had in the house. Promised to bring the rest sometime next week. Will—" She turned large sorrow filled eyes to him. "I don't think she will ever bring me the rest. I was counting on that money."

Will remembered when Lillian had delivered the blouse to Mrs. Bacher. The woman had tried the same thing, only paying for part of the value of the item. His sister had more experience in retail than Pearl. She'd been savvy enough not to leave the blouse with the woman. Pearl wasn't.

"Why did you leave the shawl with her?"

"Mrs. Bacher loved it so much. She said she was going to tell all her friends about the wonderful lace maker. That it would lead to many more orders."

"All that's true, if she does." Will placed two fingers under her chin tipping her face up.

"You don't think she will?" More tears filled Pearl's eyes.

"She probably will, but you can't count on it. Why did you leave the shawl with her?"

"What was I supposed to do? If I took it back she might not want it, and I wouldn't have even gotten the amount I did."

"And the deposit," Will said.

"That was spent on the thread."

"What? You mean you didn't get at least half the money when she placed the order, plus the cost of the thread?"

"No, I just got what I needed for the supplies. I did that wrong too, didn't I?"

Will couldn't stop himself. He pulled her against his chest. He knew she felt like a failure. He felt somewhat responsible. He and Lillian could have told her the standard procedure for a commission order. Could have told her to never deliver until the item was entirely paid for. It was something they'd learned growing up. Their grandfather and father had taught them. They never thought it was ever done any differently. Trust your client, but make sure you are paid in full before you let go of the piece.

Pearl backed away from him. "I think I'll go upstairs now. I'm not going to be very good company the rest of the day."

Will let her go and watched as she crossed the room, her shoulders slumping in defeat. He knew she was going to spend some time crying. He wanted to hold her while she did. His heart ached for her. For her disappointment. For her feelings of failure. For her tears.

Will finally admitted to himself what he'd been denying for weeks. He was in love with Pearl. There was a peace within him when she was near. Even if she was upstairs and he couldn't see her, just knowing she was there brought on that peace. He knew a house with her would be a peaceful home. She just exuded peace.

That wasn't what his home had been growing up. He loved his mother, but her intensity and determination brought with it a constant level of anxiety. It even entered the shop when she came in.

Will thought if the tone of each woman was a visible color, Pearl's would be a soft green while his mother's would be vivid orange. Both were pretty colors, but it was easier to look at the soft green for a long time. The orange was best in small doses.

Will sat down at his work bench and opened his personal drawer. At the very back was Pearl's watch-locket. He took it out and opened it. The watch had stopped so he wound it. The small second hand dial began moving and there was a soft tick, tick, tick. He closed the watch cover and opened the back. The engraving sparkled in light of the electric lamp hanging above him. *'To Pearl Henry, From Papa and Mama, Sept. 9, 1906.'*

He'd asked her once if she ever contemplated going home. Pearl had told him there was no place for her there. When she'd married, her grandparents, her father's parents, had moved in. There were several younger siblings and an older brother who was married. The couple lived in the house, too. They'd had a baby last winter. There simply was no room for her. Though Pearl never said, Will thought the family worked hard but weren't very prosperous.

He wanted to give the watch-locket back but knew she wouldn't accept it. Pearl would pay her debt to him.

So deep in thought, Will didn't hear the bell jingle when the shop door opened. Didn't hear anyone approach until his mother's voice broke into his musings.

"That's a lovely locket. Where did you get it?"

Will jerked at the sound of her voice. "It's Pearl's. It was given to her by her parents on her eighteenth birthday."

She took it from him, read the inscription, snapped the cover closed, then opened the watch side. "Have you just repaired it? It seems to be running well."

"No. It's always worked." He looked up at his mother.

"She sold it to you on the day she fainted here, didn't she?"

"Yes."

"Why isn't it out in the display case?"

"I'm not going to sell it to anyone but back to Pearl. I paid for it with my money, not the shop's." He held his hand out palm up. Luella placed the watch in it.

"Be careful, Will. Don't think more than you should about her. You may be mistaking the desire to rescue her for more than it is." The tightness in his mother's voice told Will more than her words. Will kept his face down, putting the watch back into its spot in the drawer. He didn't want his mother to see the truth in his eyes. There would be no way he could convince her that his feelings were true. That he loved Pearl because of who she was, not the circumstances of their meeting. Instead, he picked up the watch he had been cleaning when Pearl returned from delivering the shawl. That was something he could do something about.

CHAPTER NINE

Will walked into the bank and made his deposit. It was Monday. Pearl hadn't come back downstairs at all on Saturday, nor had she come to church Sunday morning. Since she had moved in with his sister, Pearl came with his sister to their church each week. When he'd inquired, Lillian had told him she wasn't feeling up to coming. Will thought it might be that she was still upset about not being paid enough for the shawl.

Lillian was at the shop and he didn't need to rush back. He had another mission. Leaving the teller window, Will went to the reception desk and requested to see Mr. Bacher.

"Hello, Mr. Miller," the bank manager said, smiling and offering his hand for Will to shake. "What can I do for you today?"

They went into his office and sat on either side of the desk. Will was uncomfortable about bringing the issue of the shawl up, but Pearl needed to be paid for her work. It certainly wasn't that Mrs. Bacher couldn't afford to pay her.

They made small talk about Will's new house, the weather, and other things going on in St. Joseph. Will turned the topic slowly. "I heard you went to the theater on Saturday evening, Mr. Bacher."

"Yes, we had a fine time." Will felt the man examine him. "Why do you ask?"

"This is very awkward, and I hate to bring it to your attention. If it was something pertaining to me, I'd just write it off, but Mrs. Ward can't afford to." Will swallowed. "Did your wife wear a new shawl to the theater?"

"Yes." There was a note of caution in the word. "It was very beautiful." Mr. Bacher paused, clasping his hands together on his desk.

"The shawl was commissioned by Mrs. Bacher to be made by Mrs. Ward. It was delivered on Saturday."

"Let me guess," Mr. Bacher said. "My wife claimed to only have part of the money to pay for it. She said she would bring the rest sometime this week." He opened a drawer and took out a check.

"Yes, Mrs. Ward came back to the shop devastated. She is a widow and works very hard to make ends meet. We sell a lot of her lacework at the shop.

"How much did my wife short Mrs. Ward?" His pen was poised to write the check. Will told him and watched him fill out the paper. "This seems to be a habit my wife has. Most merchants know not to deliver an item until they are paid in full." He took out a piece of stationary and wrote a quick note.

"Yes, Mrs. Ward is new to commission work. I plan to go over better business practices with her."

Mr. Bacher blotted both the check and note and slid them across the desk. Will glanced at the check as he picked it up. "You didn't need to write it for this amount."

"I know. It's a little bonus for the distress Mrs. Ward has undergone. Thank you for bringing this to my attention. If I guess correctly, Mrs. Ward wouldn't have."

Will folded the check and note and put them in his pocket. "No, I don't think she would have." He stood to leave. "Thank you for being so kind. It can't be easy to have someone bring such a disagreeable matter to your attention."

Mr. Bacher extended his hand. "It's not, but I've gotten

used to it over the years. Seems to be a habit for my wife. No matter how often I tell her she needs to pay the proper amount, this still occurs. I hope this doesn't sully our relationship. Bavarian Jewelry and Watch Repair has been, and is, a valued customer of the bank."

"There's no need to worry on that account. Thank you again, Mr. Bacher."

Will made one more stop before going back to the shop. He purchased a small notebook, ledger, and receipt book for Pearl. If she was going to take on commission work, learning to keep good records would help her immensely.

~~~~~

Pearl had spent all her free time making sample motifs to show Mrs. Clary and her daughter. Now she was ironing the cotton pieces before placing them in a large pouch. Lillian had made the lined draw-string bag for her to carry her crocheting in when the shawl had become too large for the one she had been using.

God had truly blessed her when she met the Millers. Their support and the opportunities they'd given her couldn't be measured. It seemed they just kept picking her up each time she fell. The latest had been what Will had done for her earlier in the week.

Pearl smiled remembering Will's delight at presenting her with the check for more than the amount due. Mr. Bacher had added some for the distress his wife had caused her, or so the note he'd enclosed with the check said.

There was one Miller who seemed not as enthusiastic in her support as she had been in the past. Mrs. Miller kept quiet when Pearl was around. She tended the shop a couple of afternoons a week so Lillian and Will could visit their father. Previously, if she came on Saturday, she would visit and encourage Pearl to keep her company until her children returned.

This past week, however, though Mrs. Miller still greeted Pearl, she didn't chat or inquire as to how her day had gone as she had before. Her silence didn't encourage Pearl to remain in the shop, so she went upstairs trying to figure out what she'd done wrong to earn Mrs. Miller's enmity.

Placing the last motif in the bag, Pearl put the flat-iron on its stand. She felt more confident going to show the samples than she ever had before. Will and Lillian had sat down with her and explained how to handle arranging for a commission as well as how to deal with difficult clients.

She now had a small notebook she would record the details of a commission in. She also had a receipt book to record each payment. Will and Lillian had told her how to keep good notes and records of the orders and payments. Each commission would be paid for in full at the time of delivery. Pearl realized this was standard business since that's the way Townsend and Wyatt handled special orders.

Pearl pinned her hat on and slipped her hands into her lace gloves, and went downstairs. "I'm off to meet with Mrs. Clary and her daughter. Pray they like my motifs and place the order. I counted the skeins of white silk at the store and they should have enough that I won't have to order it. I can begin the dress right away," she said as she passed Will sitting in his usual spot at the work bench. Lillian was rearranging a tray of brooches at the counter.

"You'll be winding little balls of thread all afternoon and evening. That's so boring. I don't know how you stand it," Lillian said with a laugh.

"Oh, I sit while I do it. Much more comfortable."

Her response brought a chuckle from Will. "If you get the commission, I'll treat you both to supper at the restaurant in the Hotel Robidoux tonight."

"Well, well, brother dear, aren't you the big spender." Lillian gave her brother an inquiring look.

"I just think we should celebrate success. Pearl's becoming a great success in the Irish lace business."

"You pray big, Lillian. I'd love to have a meal at the hotel. I've never been inside." Pearl crossed the room to the shop door, then looked back at her friend. She glanced at Will but quickly moved her eyes away. He was looking intently at her. It made her shiver inside in a way she hadn't since Patrick's illness.

Lillian saluted. "Oh, I will, but not only so we can eat out. I want you to get the commission. That wedding gown will set you up for many more orders."

The day was typical for late June, hot, sunny, and humid. Pearl took the electric trolley across town. It didn't stop in the neighborhoods where the wealthy families lived, so she walked the rest of the way. She felt a bit wilted by the time she got there. Pearl hoped they offered her a drink of water when she arrived.

The house was large and built of red brick with a wide porch the roof of which was supported by tall white columns. Gingerbread trim was painted bright white, as were the shutters. The property was surrounded by an intricate wrought iron fence. Well-tended gardens lined the walk. When her knock was answered, a uniformed butler guided her into a sitting room where Mrs. Clary and Daisy were waiting.

"Mrs. Ward, I'm so glad you have arrived. It's beastly hot outside. Here, have a glass of lemonade." Mrs. Clary poured a tall glass from a crystal pitcher.

Her hosts were gracious and loved the ideas Pearl set forth. From the many sample motifs she'd brought, Daisy picked the ones she liked the best.

"These are made from cotton, so you would be able see the designs. I'll make yours from silk thread. I already checked, and Townsend and Wyatt have enough on hand."

Daisy clapped her hands in delight. "Do you think

you'll have enough for us to see next week? I'd love to have you come back to show us."

"Yes," said Mrs. Clary. "We can confirm that Daisy likes them made from silk. I wouldn't want you to make most of them and she change her mind."

"Yes, ma'am. I can do that. There may only be one of each." Pearl jotted the designs chosen in her notebook. She began to explain some more, but the sitting room door opened and a young man came in.

"Mother— Oh, I didn't know you had company."

"Come in Guy. We are nearly finished. Daisy, please, go get my checkbook. I need to pay the deposit for your gown."

Daisy did as she was bid and Guy took her place on the settee facing where Pearl sat.

"Mrs. Ward, this is my son, Mr. Guy Clary. I dare say you will see him frequently as you come about the gown. Guy, this is Mrs. Ward. She's making the lace gown for your sister's wedding."

They made the expected greetings and Pearl began gathering the motifs scattered across the coffee table, putting them in her bag. The way Guy Clary was staring at her made Pearl uncomfortable. She hoped he wasn't around much while she was there.

Daisy was soon back, and once the check was written and safely tucked in Pearl's handbag, she stood to leave. Mr. Clary rose, too.

"I'll see you out," he said.

"There's no need," Pearl replied, pulling her lace gloves on.

"I insist." He turned to Mrs. Clary. "I came to tell you I was heading out to meet with some friends. Don't wait supper for me." Guy gave his mother a kiss on the cheek then took Pearl's arm.

When they stood on the front porch Pearl tried to remove her arm from his grasp without seeming rude.

Rather than release her, Guy slid his hand down her arm to lift her hand.

"I see you have no wedding ring," he said.

Pearl managed to pull her hand away and gathered her bag, holding it to her so he couldn't take her hand again. "I'm widowed."

A gleam appeared in his eyes that she didn't like. The wonderful commission dimmed a bit. If she had to deal with the son, coming to this house would become a chore rather than a joy.

"I'm going in my motorcar. May I take you home?" Guy smiled what might have been a charming smile, but it only made Pearl more nervous.

"Thank you for the offer, but no. I have several stops to make. I wouldn't want to inconvenience you. Goodbye." Pearl hurried down the steps and to the street. She didn't look back, not wanting to encourage the young man or reveal he made her nervous.

A few minutes later a motorcar went by. Guy Clary waved and honked the horn. Pearl just kept walking toward the trolley stop.

~~~~~

Will held the chair for Pearl while Dr. Strasser helped seat Lillian. The doctor had shown up in the shop with his watch in dire need of repair just as Will was leaving. Somehow, he couldn't exactly remember how it happened, but suddenly the doctor was joining them for supper. Will thought his sister might have engineered the entire thing.

He'd made reservations at the Hotel Robidoux for them. Only two years old, the hotel was the height of luxury. White, gray, and rose colored marble floors, walls, and even a marble water fountain on the landing of the staircase had all four of them staring in awe. The lobby furniture was upholstered in plush velvet.

The ladies were dressed in their Sunday best. Pearl's gown was coral with a wide waistband that the bodice and skirt gathered into it. The sleeves were long puffs that narrowed to cuffs just past the elbows. The high-necked bodice and sleeve cuffs were decorated with cream Irish lace. Will knew Pearl must have made the lace and added it to the rather simple gown.

Lillian was wearing a gown she'd gotten last year. It was lavender with a deeper lavender sleeveless jacket he'd heard his sister call a bolero. The bolero had small steel beads along the edge. Also, with large puff sleeves and narrow waistband, it was heavily decorated with Valenciennes lace. Will knew it was odd for a man to know different types of lace, but since he sold it in his shop the knowledge was useful.

He'd gone home early, leaving Lillian to close the shop, and changed into his suit. He'd met Dr. Strasser as he stepped off the trolley. They'd collected the ladies and walked the few blocks to the hotel.

Will watched Pearl take delight in the elegant decor and the sophisticated table settings. The room was made of deep green marble with bronze trim. The high ceiling was supported by square columns with sconces holding four electric candles each.

She touched the edge of the plate. It was white porcelain with gold scrolling around the edge. The red Robidoux crest topped the rim with evenly spaced six gold and red pineapples surrounding the center.

"I've never been in such an elegant place before," Pearl said, her eyes wide with wonder. "Thank you for bringing me here. It's something I'll always remember."

"It's fitting for our little celebration," Will touched her hand that was fingering the various forks beside her plate.

"I haven't heard what we are celebrating," Dr. Strasser said. He was sitting between Will and Lillian at the round table. Pearl was on Will's other side with Lillian next to her.

"Pearl, um, Mrs. Ward, delivered a commission shawl

last Saturday and today she accepted a commission for a lace wedding gown." Lillian beamed a smile at Pearl.

"Congratulations, Mrs. Ward," the doctor said. "You must be very pleased."

"Thank you, Dr. Strasser. I am. I never imagined I could make a living doing Irish lace crochet."

Will saw Pearl and Lillian exchange glances. It was as if they were sharing a secret.

The waiter came, poured glasses of wine, and they placed their orders. Once they were alone, Will lifted his glass. "To Pearl being successful in her crocheting endeavors." They clinked their glasses and sipped the light wine. "We are here celebrating another happy event."

Lillian and Pearl glanced at each other again, this time with concern. They definitely were keeping something from him. There was no way he could quiz his sister now. Instead, Will set his glass on the table and waved his hand asking for their attention. "I also have a commission to celebrate. Mr. Norbury is planning a party for his wife's birthday. He didn't tell me how old she will be, but he inferred it was a milestone. To mark the occasion, he has asked me to make a matched set for her. It will be platinum and diamonds. A necklace, bracelet, earrings, and tiara."

"Oh my, Will," Lillian exclaimed. "That's wonderful. Isn't it Dr. Strasser? My brother is a very talented jeweler. He creates beautiful pieces." She smiled at the doctor, then drew her eyebrows together and looked at Will. "How come I didn't know about this? You didn't tell me."

Will ran a finger around his collar. Lillian being upset wasn't always the most pleasant company. "You've been visiting father the times he's come in to discuss it. Until it was certain and the deposit made, I didn't want to say anything. That's done, and I've ordered the gems and platinum. I'll begin working on the pieces as soon as they arrive."

Pearl laid her hand on his arm drawing his attention to her. Warmth, caused by her hand, swept through his entire body. "Congratulations, Will. I'm delighted for you. We'll both be working on important orders at the same time."

"Yes, we will. I'm going to try and get caught up on all the repairs and smaller orders by the time the metal and gems arrive. I'll be able to concentrate on the set without worrying about my other customers. Plan for me to be staying late most evenings."

"And for us to feed you supper," Lillian teased. Will just grinned at her.

"Do you have the designs planned?" Pearl asked.

"I've been working on them at home in the evenings. They aren't finalized. Mr. Norbury is coming in next week, and we'll work out all the details then."

"Well, this is a celebration, indeed," Dr. Strasser said. "I'd like to mark this auspicious occasion by asking you all to include me within your friendship and call me by my given name, Vernon. I feel sort of left out being called Dr. Strasser when you are more familiar with your address to each other."

Will watched Lillian beam her brilliant smile at Vernon. Hum… is that the way the wind was blowing? Did their mother know?

"I believe that is a marvelous idea. We can be Vernon, Will, Pearl, and Lillian to each other." Lillian settled herself more comfortably in her chair as if punctuating the declaration.

Will looked at Pearl. She was smiling at Dr. Strasser, Vernon. That didn't settle well on Will. His insides tightened. He looked at the man sitting next to him. Vernon had his eyes fixed on Lillian, smiling at her. The knot in his chest loosened as he saw his sister blush and drop her eyes to her lap.

"I have an idea," Vernon said, leaning forward a little with his eagerness. "The Fourth of July is a week from

Monday. I hear they are having some special events at Lake Contrary Amusement Park. The four of us could spend the day. What do you say?"

Before Will could reply, Lillian and Pearl both squealed in delight then giggled as those sitting at nearby tables looked at them.

CHAPTER TEN

Pearl followed Lillian down the stairs. Her friend was very excited about the day ahead. It was the Fourth of July and they were being escorted by Will and Dr. Strasser, Vernon, to the Amusement Park at Lake Contrary. Lillian hadn't stopped talking about the event for the past week. She had found all the advertisements concerning the celebrations and cut them all out of the newspaper. Every ride and concession was studied and discussed. She had planned out the order in which they would be ridden, where she thought they might like to eat, and what games she wanted to try and watch the men try.

"This is the first year we haven't spent at least part of the day with family, though I guess I am since Will is going with us. I was so surprised when Father and Mother announced last Sunday that they were traveling to Hot Springs, Arkansas so Father can take the waters. Weren't you? And so soon. They tell us on Sunday and leave on Friday. I couldn't believe Vernon didn't say anything to me at all about it. You'd have thought he'd let me know. I think he knows I'm peeved at him. He hasn't called or dropped by all week. Do you think he'll not come today? He must know I'm upset with him for not telling me. I'd hate for him to stand me up. That would ruin my day completely."

Lillian opened her mouth to say more as Pearl caught up with her, but Pearl placed her fingers on her friend's lips. "Shhh. I know you were upset with your parents' decision to travel, but Vernon couldn't say anything about it if he knew: physician-patient confidentiality." She dropped her hand. "I'm pretty sure he never gave how you would feel a single thought. Men don't think the way we do."

"I'm sure you are right." Lillian stepped to the mirror hanging on the wall, pulled the pin from her hat and inserted it again. "I don't want to lose this hat. The egret feathers were very— well, let's just say, Mother would have her own apoplectic fit if she knew what I spent on them. The milliner wanted to put the entire bird on the crown, but I don't want a dead bird on my head. It does go well with my dress, don't you think? I'm so glad Mr. Dimmick made me purchase the dress fabric. This new style is so much more practical. I don't need as many petticoats. That it only goes down to the ankle instead of the floor is so much nicer, too. Much better to show off one's shoes." She stepped away, allowing Pearl to check herself in the mirror.

"Thank you, Lillian, for remaking my dress. There's no way I could have made the adjustments you did to bring the style up to date."

"You're welcome. Thank you for the gloves. You didn't need to make them for me." Lillian pulled the gloves on then placed her finger on a pleat in Pearl's bodice. "I'll be able to let these tucks out when you begin to show."

Both ladies were in white, which was in fashion for the summer months. Lillian's straw hat was new with stylish plumes. Pearl's was decorated with a spray of lace she'd made.

The shop door opened admitting Will and Vernon. Dapper looking in their linen suits and straw hats, both men wore wide smiles.

"Greetings, ladies. You both look lovely, today," Will said.

Pearl couldn't resist. "Inferring we do not always look lovely, so it must be noted?"

Will's face turned bright red. He stammered and looked at Pearl, then shifted his gaze to Vernon and Lillian.

Stepping past him, Lillian patted Will on the chest. "Don't worry, brother. She's teasing you. Your compliment was lovely in itself. Thank you."

"Yes, Will," Pearl touched his arm. "It was. Thank you."

"So," Vernon began, "are we ready to go to the Park?"

"It will be a while for the trolley to come by." Lillian looked at the large clock on the wall. "Wait. You shouldn't be here yet. The trolley won't be by for another twenty minutes."

Vernon grinned. "We aren't going by trolley. I took delivery of my motorcar this week. It's a touring car so will hold all four of us."

"You bought a motorcar?" Lillian squealed. "Where is it? Can I drive?" She raced to the door and threw it open, heading out to the street. By the time the rest exited the building, and Will locked the door, Lillian was seated behind the wheel. "Crank it on, Vernon."

The doctor stood next to the vehicle with his hands on his hips. "I don't think so, Lillian. It's harder than it looks to drive. I'm still learning myself and don't feel confident to teach you."

"Besides," Will mumbled to Pearl. "It's brand new. She's liable to crash it. I doubt Vernon wants that to happen."

Pearl grinned and nodded. She couldn't take her eyes off the motorcar. A Ford Model T Touring Car, it was deep green with two black leather upholstered seats. The roof was folded down behind the rear seat. Brass lanterns sat just below the windshield, and more brass trimmed the covering of the motor.

"I've never ridden in a motorcar," Pearl said. She flashed a broad smile at Vernon and Will. "How do I get in?"

"This way, m'lady." Will turned a handle and opened the door to the rear seat. "Allow me to help you alight."

She smiled at him and extended her hand. Pearl glanced at Vernon once she was seated. He was arguing with Lillian, trying to get her to slide to the right so he could sit behind the wheel. When she finally moved he jumped in. Will was standing in front of the car. He bent over and cranked the handle. The motor sputtered, coughed, and then began to run. Will ran around to climb in next to Pearl.

"Is everyone ready?" Vernon asked.

"Go!" Lillian said.

He shifted the gear and they pulled away from the curb. As excited as she was to ride in the horseless carriage, Pearl clutched the side of the car with one hand and gripped Will's with the other.

~~~~~

The six miles they traveled to Lake Contrary seemed to fly by and drag at the same time for Pearl. Although she'd ridden on trains, she'd never gone so fast out in the open before. The buildings, then the houses and landscapes passed by in nearly a blur. Her grip on the door and Will's hand tightened each time they went around a corner. What if the motorcar fell over? They were going so fast.

Vernon drove onto the grass and stopped. The engine quit, and he turned in his seat so he could look in the rear seat and see Lillian too.

"So, what do you think? Did you enjoy the ride?" Vernon asked.

"It was dilly." Lillian was beaming her delight. "When are you going to let me drive?"

"Not any time soon," was Vernon's reply. "Come on.

Let's go have some more fun." Vernon jumped out of the car and ran around to assist Lillian down while Will did the same for Pearl.

"I've never been to Lake Contrary Amusement Park," Pearl said, as Will tucked her hand in the crook of his elbow. "Lillian told me about it. It sounds like you have pleasant memories of coming here as a child."

"Not to the amusement park, as that's a recent addition. The area has been used for recreation for a long while though. We came here some for bathing in the lake and picnicking." Will pointed to their right. "The horse racing track has been here the longest. The grandstand was built about ten years ago. Father and I came here on occasion. Mother didn't approve, but we came anyway. She'd give us stern looks when we got home but never made a large issue of it. Father didn't gamble on the horses. We just liked watching them race."

"Oh, look," Lillian exclaimed. "I can see the Shoot the Chutes ride. I do so want to do that. It's new, just opening this year. Let's do that first." She tugged on Vernon's arm wanting him to move faster.

The roof of the ride was just visible over the trees. When they reached the midway, they could see many of the offerings of the park. To their left was a building advertising lunch and ice cream. Further on was a building housing a penny arcade, various concessions, and a pool hall. Bisecting the midway was a long lagoon. At the far end was a tall incline. A foot bridge crossed just where the incline met the water. It was crowded with spectators.

Just then, a sled shot down the incline and splashed into the water. Squeals, shrieks, and laughter could be heard as they approached the end of the lagoon.

"Oh, I so want to do that. Can we go now?" Lillian was fairly jumping in her excitement.

Pearl smiled but eyed the ride with suspicion. Will must

have noted her wariness.

"How about we stroll some more and see what else is here? Look." He pointed right. "There's the Merry-Go-Round. I heard all the animals have real horse-hair tails."

They wandered toward the octagonal structure. Vernon veered to a small booth, turning Lillian over to her brother. "I'll be right back."

He rejoined them as they stood watching the carousel go around. "I can't believe they had these. They are new, only a couple years old. I've read about them. These candies are taking the country by storm." He passed out small wrapped nuggets.

Pearl looked at the paper. "Tootsie Roll." She unwrapped the candy and found a small dark brown cylinder. Taking a bite, she smiled. "Oh my, that is so good. Chocolate," she exclaimed, not caring that she was speaking with her mouth full.

"Yummy." Lillian popped the rest of the confection into her mouth. When she'd swallowed, she said, "Let's make sure to buy some to take home before we leave."

"Good idea," Vernon said. "But we may want to purchase them early, as I'm sure they will sell out."

They continued along the south side of the midway past the Figure Eight Roller Coaster and the Old Mill Waterway Ride. Pearl noticed a sly grin pass between Will and Vernon. What was that about?

"Come on." Lillian tugged on Vernon's arm. "Let's go on the bridge and watch the boats come down the chute. Then, I want to do it. If the rest of you are too chicken to try, I'll go by myself."

Pearl was getting caught up in her friend's excitement. They stood in the middle of the bridge, first watching the boats slide down the incline, gaining speed before they disappeared under the bridge. The squeals coming from the passengers made them all laugh.

They turned and crossed to the other railing just as a

boat splashed into the water, spraying the liquid out in front of them.

"It does look like fun," Pearl said. "I've never done anything like it before."

"Do you want to get in line now? Or do some of the other rides first? They may seem tame after Shooting the Chutes?" Will asked.

"Oh," Lillian exclaimed. "I hadn't thought of that. Maybe we should do the Merry-Go-Round and the Old Mill Water Way ride first."

They decided to walk some more and found the baseball diamond as they rounded the end of the roller coaster. A sign said there would be a game beginning in a couple of hours.

The aroma of fried chicken drew them to the Cottage Inn, directly behind the Merry-Go-Round. Their mouths watered and they decided to ride the carousel then eat some of the chicken that had a reputation of being some of the best in St. Joe.

~~~~~

Will held Pearl's hand as she stepped onto the platform of the Merry-Go-Round. He was enjoying having her at his side. So far, the day had exceeded his expectations. Her fear during the drive out to the Park was still evident in his sore fingers. Maybe he'd place his arm around her shoulders when they rode back to town. That would make her feel more secure, surely.

The horse she chose was white with a colorful red and pink painted mane. It was also stopped at the top of its vertical cycle. Will grinned and placed his hands on Pearl's waist. "Here, let me help you." Before she could protest or choose a different horse, Will lifted her up into the saddle. She teetered a little as she settled side-saddle and took hold of the brass pole. His horse was to the inside of hers and was black with a white mane. Just as he mounted, the music volume increased and the ride began its circular path.

Will watched Pearl as their horses moved up and down. Was it too soon to let her know of his interest in her? That he wanted to court her. That he was already planning a future with her. She'd only been widowed three months.

Propriety dictated that she be in mourning for a year before pursuing another relationship. That was if anyone else knew about it. Maybe he could indicate his interest and they could spend the next months learning more about each other and eventually begin making plans for after her period of mourning was over.

Her eyes met his occasionally as she looked avidly around. They echoed the smile on her face. He was glad to see her relaxed and having a good time. It seemed she'd been more somber and serious lately. Something was concerning her. He wanted to inquire but since neither she or Lillian had mentioned anything, he kept his peace. Maybe it was just grief due to the loss of her husband. He hoped that was all it was.

The ride slowed and finally stopped. Will's horse was higher than Pearl's now. He jumped down just as she stood. They ended up close together because of the small space.

"You're supposed to dismount from a horse on the left, sir," Pearl teased.

"And miss the opportunity to be this close to a beautiful lady? I think not." He watched color infuse her cheeks. Grabbing her hand he led her to the edge of the platform and helped her descend.

Vernon, with Lillian on his arm, met them at the exit. "We beat you in the race," he laughed.

Lillian swatted his arm. "We were just ahead of them on the ride. It wasn't a race."

Vernon lifted her hand to his lips and kissed the back of it. "It is if I say so, and I do, and we won."

Will exchanged a look with Pearl, whose eyebrow was raised slightly as was one corner of her mouth. Maybe he'd have to quiz her on his sister's interest in the young doctor. That he could do without crossing the boundary of propriety. She was his sister. It was his job to watch out for her, to say nothing of his job to butt into her life.

The fried chicken was every bit as good as its reputation proclaimed. It was served with potato salad and other picnic sorts of foods. They decided to forego dessert as they all wanted to try the ice cream later in the afternoon.

A crier announced the baseball game was to commence shortly, so they procured tickets in the grandstand so the ladies wouldn't have to sit in the sun. Since they didn't care which team won, they cheered for both.

A couple of young boys hawked Cracker Jack, so the men bought two boxes and shared the sweet popcorn with the ladies. When the crowd began singing 'Take Me Out To The Ballgame,' Will and Vernon held up their boxes showing that they'd bought some 'peanuts and Cracker Jack' since Will had run to the stand before the game began, saying, "I can't watch a baseball game without something to snack on."

~~~~~

"Let's either get ice cream or ride those rides," Lillian pointed to the building where ice cream was sold, then to the Shoot the Chutes and the roller coaster. "The lines aren't getting any shorter."

Pearl looked and saw she was right. The lines for both rides would mean standing and waiting. "We could get the ice cream and eat it while we wait in line. They are selling it in paper bowls. I've seen quite a few people with them eating with little wooden sticks. See." She indicated three children sitting on a bench, each with a small bowl. The youngest had dripped chocolate ice cream down the front of his white shirt.

They split up, the men going to get the ice cream, the women taking the opportunity to go to the ladies' room before they got in line for the roller coaster. Lillian said she wanted to save the Chute for last.

When they were in the ladies' retiring room, Lillian studied Pearl's face. "Are you doing well? I don't want you to get too tired. Just say the word and I'll make an excuse to leave."

Pearl set her hand on Lillian's arm. "I'm doing okay. Sitting for the baseball game was restful. I'm sure I'll be tired when we head home, but I want to stay for as long as we planned. I want to see the fireworks even though I know it will be late when we leave. I'm having so much fun. I haven't had as much fun since before Patrick took ill."

Lillian squeezed Pearl's hand. "I understand. You just let me know if you want to rest, though. We can find a place under the trees and send the men off to play in the penny arcade or the pool hall for a while. So long as they don't go to the cigar shack or the beer garden. Cigars stink and beer makes men muddle headed," Lillian said with disgust, making Pearl laugh.

"Come, let's get in line. The men will be coming with our ice cream." Pearl led the way to where the line for the roller coaster began. The men joined them and they ate their cold treat as they watched the cars race around the track. "Are you sure they won't fly off? They go so fast." Pearl watched the car filled with screaming riders hurtle past. She was unsure if she wanted to climb in one and whip around the figure eight.

Will must have picked up on her unease. "It's safe. Look at the way the wheels are on the tracks. They can't go off the rails." He grinned at her. "I'll be next to you and hold you in. Does that make you feel safer?"

Pearl was surprised that it did. That Will would make sure she was safe. Patrick had been like that— supportive but not suppressive. "Yes, it does. Thank you." She licked the last bit of ice cream off the stick. "Thank you for the ice cream too, and all the other things you've bought me today. I did bring money to pay my own way."

Will took the bowl and stick. "No need. Today is my treat." He smiled and went to toss the trash in the barrel nearby.

True to his word, Will sat next to her in the car. When the attendant fastened the bar across their laps, he wrapped his arm around her taking hold of the bar, enclosing her in his embrace.

She looked at him, and the emotion in his eyes made her stomach flutter. When the car began moving as the chain pulled it up the incline, Pearl gripped the bar harder and looked forward.

With a clank, clank, clank the car rose to the top. It paused a second then dropped over the edge. A scream rose as Pearl's stomach was left at the top to follow as the car zoomed down then around a curve, back up another smaller incline, and down again. Around, up, down, around it went until it slowed and stopped at the place they boarded the car.

"You have to let go now, Pearl," Will whispered in her ear. "It's time to get off."

Will studied her face. She tried to smile at him but knew he saw through her. This was not something she wanted to ever do again. It was too fast, too rough a ride, and her stomach was still trying to catch up with the rest of her body.

As he helped her out, Lillian came close and grabbed Pearl's hand. "Wasn't it wonderful? That was so much fun. I want to do it again, but I want to Shoot the Chutes first. Then, we can come back and get in line again. Come on. Let's hurry to get in line." She ran off, grabbing Vernon's hand and dragging him toward the people waiting to Shoot the Chute.

Pearl and Will followed more slowly. She re-secured her hat and took a deep breath. "Your sister is quite adventurous."

Will chuckled. "Yes, she always has been. She was a tomboy when she was growing up. She climbed trees, the porch trellis, onto the outhouse roof, which caved in. That didn't make Mother or Father very happy. It did instigate the installation of the indoor plumbing of the house. We all enjoyed that."

Pearl laughed. "Do you think Vernon will allow her to drive his motorcar?"

"Not soon, I'm sure, and if he does, he should do it way out in the country where there aren't pedestrians or other vehicles close by. I fear she would drive much faster than she should."

"No doubt."

Lillian and Vernon were arguing about the same topic when they joined them in line. Lillian was begging to be allowed to drive at least partway home with Vernon staunch in his refusal.

"You're an old stick in the mud," Lillian complained.

"Better me stuck in the mud than my brand new motorcar." Vernon turned from facing her to watching the sled splash into the lagoon.

"Uh oh," Will whispered in Pearl's ear. "Trouble between them. Lillian better be careful or he'll not want to see her again."

"She'd be devastated if that happened. She truly cares for him, though I'd deny saying so if asked." Pearl winked at Will.

~~~~~

Will helped Pearl into the shallow sled-like boat. It would be pulled up the incline using the same type of mechanism as the roller coaster. Here, however, there was no bar to be secured over their laps. Pearl gripped his knee as the boat ascended the incline. He didn't think she even realized it. When her fingers tightened he pried them off and held them.

"You are not as adventurous as Lillian," he whispered. The four of them were seated in one seat in the boat with the ladies in the middle. He shifted her hand to his other one and wrapped his arm around her.

"What was your first clue?" Pearl whispered back. One hand clung to his hand while the other clutched the seat of the bench they were sitting on.

They reached the top and looked down the long steep slide that ended in the lagoon below. With a shove to the back of the boat, over the edge they went.

The shriek in his ear nearly deafened him. Pearl leaned against him as they rushed down. Then darkness for a moment as they went under the bridge into the lagoon with a great whoosh of water.

"Oh my, that was so much fun. I want to do it again."

Will looked at Pearl, surprised at her words. They sounded as if they'd come from Lillian. Her eyes twinkled with joy and excitement.

Pearl turned away and hugged Lillian. "Let's go again. That was so much fun."

Lillian laughed, agreeing.

Will looked over at Vernon who grinned and shrugged.

They went down the Chute several more times, with Lillian and Vernon splitting their time with it and the roller coaster.

Will and Pearl strolled along the Midway's concessions. He purchased them each a bottle of iced soda while they waited for Lillian and Vernon to take 'One last roller coaster ride. Please, Vernon, please.'

Will wished he'd purchased one of Kodak Camera's new Brownie cameras so he could take Pearl's photograph as she sipped her ginger ale through a straw. It would have made a wonderful memory of the day.

Pearl looked up at him, and he noted the fatigue in her eyes. Once again, Will became concerned about her health. Was something wrong? Was she ailing? It was impolite to ask, so he kept quiet.

When Lillian and Vernon met them under the shade of the old oak trees, he looked at Lillian. She was a little wilted from the heat and all the rides she had ridden but didn't have the overall tired look Pearl did. The plan had been to stay until the fireworks display over the lake but that wouldn't be until dark, several hours away. They had reservations for supper at the Lotus Club. Should they forego those activities and take the ladies home? Pearl had to work all day tomorrow and the rest of the week.

"We have a ride we haven't tried yet," Lillian said just before she took a sip of her Coca-Cola. "Although after the roller coaster and the Chute, if might seem tame."

Will looked at her.

"The Old Mill Waterway. It looks to be inside and might be cool and refreshing after all this time in the sun. Although you have found a nice shady spot. Besides, the line isn't long like at the other rides. What do you say?"

Pearl's smile convinced him she was game for the idea. Maybe he could think of some way to allow them all to relax a while before they ate supper. He could also suggest that they drive the motorcar to the club. That would save the walk there and back after the fireworks.

Will didn't know what to expect when they entered the building. He wasn't surprised it was a boat ride. The name gave that away. It was the boats themselves. Some were low and wide with several seats. Others were narrow, with a high back, they were small and only seated two people. Lillian and Vernon got into the first boat. Will could see they had to sit very close together. He raised an eyebrow when Vernon placed his arm along the back of the seat.

As he settled next to Pearl, Will noted why his friend had done so. Their shoulders would be squeezed together if he didn't do the same. Not that he minded, but he didn't want Pearl to be uncomfortable.

She looked at him when he placed his arm behind her. He shrugged his shoulder. "I know you aren't going to fall out and aren't scared. There just doesn't seem to be enough room."

"It's fine."

The boat began moving with the current and entered a darkened tunnel. The walls were decorated as if it was a floral arbor. Artificial trees, vines, and flowers. Stuffed birds were in set in the trees. Light filtered in, creating a romantic atmosphere. Now Will knew why some groups were placed in the low boats with several rows of seats and why Lillian and Vernon, and he and Pearl had these narrow boats with the high backs. It was to allow courting couples a few minutes of privacy.

Pearl was gazing around at the scenery which was changing subtly as they progressed along. Will was watching her. He wanted to turn her face to him with his fingers on her chin. His lips ached to press hers and taste of her sweetness. But he didn't. She was only three months from having lost her husband. His respect for her would not allow him to breach her trust. The time would come when he could reveal his feelings for her. Now was not the time.

CHAPTER ELEVEN

Pearl rang the doorbell of the Clary home and waited for the butler to answer. She had all the sample motifs made in the silk thread, as well as drawings of the placements and sketches of the connecting stitches she planned to use. Daisy and Mrs. Clary would be making the final decisions today. The dressmaker had brought Daisy's measurements to the shop, leaving them with Lillian earlier in the week.

Pearl grinned remembering the look on Lillian's face when they exited the boats at the end of the Old Mill Waterway ride. Pearl had a feeling Vernon had taken advantage of the privacy and the romantic setting and given her friend at least one kiss. Lillian's face had been flushed, and there was a dreamy look on her face. Even knowing the inappropriateness, Pearl couldn't help but wish that Will had done the same.

The door opened, but it wasn't the butler standing there. "Good morning, Mrs. Ward," Guy said. His smile and the look in his eyes caused a shiver to run up Pearl's spine.

"Good morning, Mr. Clary. I'm to meet Mrs. and Miss Clary to discuss the wedding gown."

"Yes, so they informed me at breakfast. Do come in. They are in Mother's sitting room." He pushed the screen door open allowing Pearl to enter the foyer.

"Thank you." She walked past him.

He took her arm, slowing her progress. "Permit me to

escort you, Mrs. Ward." The emphasis he placed on her name made her uneasy. Was he inferring that he doubted her honorific?

"I'm sure I can find my way." Pearl tried to pull her arm from his grasp without drawing his attention.

"I insist. Come."

Pearl walked by his side as far from him as possible with his hand on her forearm. When they reached the open doorway to the sitting room, she was able to move away from him.

"Mrs. Clary, Miss Clary, it is delightful to see you again." Pearl ignored Mr. Clary hoping he would simply leave, but he followed her into the room. "I've brought the motifs and designs."

As she arranged them on the coffee table, Pearl felt his eyes on her. Daisy began exclaiming over the motifs, picking up several and handing them to her mother.

"Please sit, Mrs. Ward," Mrs. Clary said, and asked if Pearl would like some refreshment. As she reached for a bell to call the butler she noticed her son standing near the door. "Is there something you want, Guy? I'm sure there is nothing here that interests you."

Pearl saw his eyes flit to her then back to his mother. "Just watching my sister's delight in planning her wedding, Mother."

The look on Mrs. Clary's face showed Pearl she didn't believe his words. She looked at Pearl who concentrated on pointing out several variations possible for the bodice of the gown to Daisy.

Mrs. Clary cleared her throat. "Well, I'm sure you have more important things to do. I know your father is expecting you at the company today. He mentioned it at breakfast."

Guy bowed slightly. "Yes, Mother, I'll be leaving shortly. I have several things to accomplish first. With that in mind, I bid you adieu until later."

Pearl felt his gaze again but didn't look up. She was afraid Mrs. Clary would not like the interest her son was paying to her. She was counting on this commission to pave the way for more. It would be devastating if she lost it because of unwanted attention.

Not more than an hour later mother and daughter had decided on the motifs and designs. They scheduled Pearl to return in a few weeks with the bodice for a fitting. As they entered the hall, Guy was descending the staircase.

"Ah, have you concluded your meeting? I hope everything went well." He tugged on the cuff of his white linen suit coat and picked up a straw hat from a side table.

"Oh, yes, Guy," Daisy said. "Mrs. Ward does beautiful work. She is quite talented."

Pearl pulled on her lace gloves, keeping her focus on her hands.

"I'm sure Mrs. Ward is talented in many things," he said. Again, there was emphasis on her honorific. Pearl hoped neither Mrs. Clary or Daisy noticed it.

She looked at Mrs. Clary. "I will telephone you when I have the bodice ready for fitting and we can set up a Saturday for me to come."

"Yes, Mrs. Ward. That will be fine."

Pearl made her goodbyes and left the house. She hurried toward the trolley stop. She hoped Mr. Clary was detained by his mother or sister so she could board the trolley before he came by in his motorcar. She didn't want to give him the opportunity to stop and speak with her, which she was afraid he might do.

~~~~~

Will looked at the watch-locket in his hand. He should be working on one of the watches needing repair or cleaning. They needed to be done before the gems and platinum arrived, which should be within a week, absolutely no longer than two. Instead, he'd taken Pearl's watch-locket out of the drawer and was just sitting there looking at it.

Will was still worried about her. He thought back to the Fourth of July. They'd all had such a good time. Their meal at the Lotus Club was superb and filled most of the time before the fireworks display. Vernon had moved the motorcar, parking it facing the lake so they not only had a great view but a comfortable place to sit.

Will frowned as his concern returned. He couldn't believe what had happened during the fireworks. In the middle of all the explosions, Pearl had leaned against him, her head resting on his shoulder. At first his heart had raced, thinking she was showing an interest in him. Then, he'd realized she had fallen asleep. How could anyone fall asleep with all the noise from the fireworks?

She hadn't woken up until they arrived back at the shop. Even then, Pearl had to be shaken to wake up. Lillian and Pearl had laughed it off as just being tired from a long day in the sun. Will wasn't so sure.

Then on Saturday, Pearl had gone to the Clary's to speak with the mother and daughter about the wedding dress. She'd been so excited. When she returned, the anxiety she'd exhibited before was back. Pearl had gone upstairs and stayed until Lillian and he had come up for lunch. She hadn't talked much about the meeting, only saying the motifs and design were chosen and she would make the bodice, letting Mrs. and Miss Clary know when it was ready for fitting. When Lillian had quizzed her about the house, Pearl gave a rather uninspired description of the place.

Will had expressed his concern to Lillian, but she'd brushed it off, saying Pearl was simply tired and stressed from working all week and the very important meeting that morning.

Will heard his sister's footsteps coming down the stairs. He placed the watch-locket in the back of the drawer and closed it. Picking up the watch he was cleaning, Will pretended to be concentrating on his work.

"I've brought our lunch down, as you requested. I know you are busy, wanting to complete so much work before you start on the commission pieces, but I don't understand why you can't even come up for a few minutes and eat. You do know it makes more work for me. I have to make the food, plate it, carry it down here to eat. Then, I have to carry all the dishes back upstairs so I can wash them. Don't you want to get out of that chair for a while? Move around a little. Stretch your legs. You've been sitting all morning."

"No, I haven't. I've had several customers and sold several pieces of jewelry and lace. Pearl should be pleased. All the lace that sold was hers."

Lillian smiled and set the tray on the workbench. "That's good. Look, I've made a new Jell-O dessert. It's orange Jell-O, peaches, their juice, and whipped cream. Doesn't it look good? I thought the recipe looked yummy when I found it in one of my ladies magazines. I can't remember which one. I cut it out."

Lillian chattered on while they ate. When she mentioned Pearl, Will decided to bring up his concerns.

"Lillian," he interrupted her. "Is there something wrong with Pearl? Is she ill? Does she need to go to a doctor?"

Lillian straightened in her chair, a sure sign she was nervous and probably concealing something. "No, why do you ask? She's fine. Healthy as a horse, really."

Will swiveled so he was facing her. "I've noticed that she's been anxious, worried, and much more fatigued than when she first moved in. It seems to be getting worse, at least the anxiety."

"I don't know what you mean." Lillian studied her plate rather than look at him. Another sign she was hiding something. She was a terrible liar and had great difficulty keeping a secret.

Will reached out and placed his hand on her arm.

"Lillian, I care about Pearl. I need to know what is wrong."

"Please, Will. I promised I wouldn't say anything. At least, not yet."

"So, there is something wrong."

"Not really wrong, just unfortunate. It makes her life so much more complicated. She can't go home to Ohio. There's no room for her there. She's all alone and trying so hard to support herself. That's why she works so hard on the lace. She needs it to sell. Needs to build up her business by getting high paying commissions."

"But she has her job at Townsend and Wyatt. That pays her enough to cover her bills, doesn't it?"

"For now, but when she loses it." Lillian covered her mouth, stopping the words. Her chattiness had caused her to reveal more than she intended, and Will was going to take advantage of it.

"Why is she going to lose her job? I thought she was doing well as a sales clerk."

Lillian looked at the remains of her meal, the Jell-O dessert forgotten.

Will tried to think of some reason why Lillian was sure Pearl was going to lose her job. The dry goods store was popular and had a loyal cliental. He thought they did well. They were always looking for sales clerks. The women who worked there were young and mainly single. Most stayed employed there until they married. Those who remained working after they wed only left when they became in the family way.

The thought paralyzed Will. He'd never given the idea consideration. He knew little about women in that condition, but his older sisters had been so several times. Josey was expecting right now. He remembered both women complaining how fatigued they were the first few months. Pearl had been so tired lately. She'd overslept one morning and napped most Saturday afternoons. Sundays too, possibly. Pearl went to church, and often came to dinner at the Miller family home, but seldom stayed for the afternoon. She'd fallen asleep during the fireworks.

"How far along is she?" Will asked, quietly.

"Nearly four months." Lillian admitted in defeat.

"She'll begin to show soon then."

"I'm surprised she hasn't already, as thin as she is. When she does, Pearl will be let go at Townsend and Wyatt. What she's making from her lace won't begin to cover what it takes to support herself, let alone a baby."

No wonder she was anxious, Will thought. Pearl knew what it was to not have any money. That's how they had met.

Will rubbed his face. Poor Pearl. She had to be scared, knowing she was going to lose her source of income. Knowing she would have to rely on the sale of her lace. The other ladies who sold lace in the shop did so for supplemental income, not the sole source of the money they lived on.

"Please, Will. I promised I wouldn't say anything. I've broken that promise. Please don't tell Pearl," Lillian besieged him.

"I won't. At least, not yet. It will come out soon anyway. Maybe by then I'll have figured a way to help her."

~~~~~

Pearl breathed a sigh of relief. Two positive things had occurred. One, she still had her job at Townsend and Wyatt. Her waist was thickening but not so much to be noticeable yet. Within a month she would either need to quit or Mr. Dimmick would realize her condition and remove her from her position.

He'd been much nicer since she'd made the bed jacket for his wife. Pearl had practiced the motifs and connection stitches for the wedding gown by using them in the design of the bed jacket. Mr. Dimmick thought the garment was lovely and was very pleased it had been completed so quickly. Pearl hoped she would find a way to return to her job after the baby was older, and staying on Mr. Dimmick's good side was part of that goal.

The second positive thing was that Mr. Guy Clary was not evident when Pearl took the bodice to be fitted. The garment was now ready to be seamed together and the skirt begun. That would take longer since it was so much bigger and more involved. The motifs would begin small at the waist and increase gradually in size as they descended to the hem and on the train.

The late July day was sunny and promised to be hot. That was why the fitting had been so early in the morning. Pearl had arrived shortly after breakfast. Daisy's delight in the bodice pleased her. Mrs. Clary smiled affectionately as her daughter exclaimed over its beauty. The three women had shared glasses of cold lemonade on the wide porch that surrounded three sides of the house when the fitting was done.

Pearl crossed the street as she walked to the trolley stop.

"Mrs. Ward, you are looking lovely today, as usual." At the sound of Guy Clary's voice, the smile on Pearl's face faded. He was leaning against a large Maple tree, obviously lying in wait for her since he'd been hidden by the trunk until she walked passed.

"Thank you, Mr. Clary." Pearl kept walking.

Mr. Clary fell into step beside her. "Mrs. Ward." There was that slight inflection as he said her name that made Pearl think he didn't believe the honorific was correct. "I was wondering if you and I could take lunch together? There's a fine little place overlooking the river. Quite private where we could get to know each other better."

Pearl never looked at him. "I'm sorry Mr. Clary. It's impossible. Thank you for the offer."

"Oh, Mrs. Ward." His tone was sickeningly sweet. "I don't think it's as impossible as you say." Guy picked up her left hand. "I don't see a ring on this finger. I'm not even sure there ever has been. So, you see, I know what 'calling' it is that has you calling yourself Mrs. Ward."

Pearl stopped in her tracks and faced him. "Mr. Clary, you know nothing about me but my name and that I am making the lace gown for your sister's wedding. I am not interested in your advances. My circumstances are none of your business. I will give you one bit of information which you can easily verify." Pearl felt tears rising, making it difficult to get the words out. "You can find my husband by taking a right lane, then left, right again in Mount Mora cemetery. He's near the road at the back. His name is Patrick Ward. The date of his death is April 11, 1910. You go tell him you just made an improper suggestion to his widow. Good day, Mr. Clary."

Pearl was shaking as she marched away from him. How dare he infer she was a woman of low moral character. How dare he assume she had never been married and was engaged in an illicit line of work. She wiped the tears that slipped down, escaping as she tried to blink them away.

Oh, how she missed Patrick. Missed his smile. The way he would grab her around the waist when he returned from work and kiss her until she was breathless. His endless teasing about how she burned the first meal she ever cooked for him. The tender way he loved her in the night.

Pearl sat on the bench at the trolley stop. Uncertainty and fear warred within her. Would Mr. Clary say anything to his mother about how she had spoken to him? Would she lose her commission? Would he badmouth her work even if she did complete the gown? Would anyone care that a man didn't like his sister's wedding gown?

That last thought made Pearl grin. As if his opinion on how his sister looked at her wedding would matter to any woman with the means to place a special order for her lace. The grin faded. It would matter if he made aspersions on her character.

Pearl's shoulders slumped. There was nothing she could do to prevent him from doing so. She was going to lose her job at the mercantile, and now she'd made an enemy of the son of an influential client. All she could do was pray he hadn't taken offense at her rejection and begin spreading lies about her around St. Joe.

As the trolley approached, Pearl dug out the coins she needed to pay the fare to take her back downtown to the shop.

CHAPTER TWELVE

"Mrs. Ward, would you please close out your cash register and come to my office fifteen minutes before closing?" Mr. Dimmick asked.

Pearl looked up from sorting skeins of embroidery floss a child had mixed together while the mother shopped. "Yes, sir. I'll be there promptly."

She watched him walk away. Could this week get any worse? It seemed that every woman brought their ill-behaved child into the fabrics department. She supposed it was just about to. Multiple times a day she was sorting, picking up, or gently removing items from small hands.

The day had finally come, she was sure. This would be her last day at Townsend and Wyatt. It seemed as if overnight her stomach had increased in size. Yesterday, she'd had to move the buttons on the waistband of the skirt she wore to work. Today, it was tighter again.

Pearl had known this day was coming. She had ever since she'd realized she was expecting. Now that it was here, she realized she would miss the job. As much as her feet hurt by the end of the day, Pearl enjoyed helping her customers. Her knowledge of fabrics, flosses, and yarns had increased too. That would serve her well in the future as she branched out into more specialty laces. She might even try some other types of lace making.

Pearl eyed the display of crochet cottons and silks. She would purchase as much as she could afford before she lost her employee discount. She would have more time now to crochet. A lot more time. The thought both pleased and depressed her.

Her last sale was to herself. Pearl had taken the opportunity of her last break to run to her bank and take out enough money to pay for the threads she wanted to purchase. The amount she left on the shelves would not last long, so she wrote up an order for replacing all that she had bought.

With a word to the sales clerk in the next department, Pearl gathered her handbag and all the items in her small cubby in the ladies' employee lounge. She wouldn't be coming back. With one last look around, Pearl went to Mr. Dimmick's office.

"Come in and have a seat, please, Mrs. Ward." Mr. Dimmick stood as she entered the small room. He gave her a sad smile. "First, my wife loves her bed jacket. She even wears it when she isn't confined to the bed. I'm hoping you will consent to making a warmer one for the winter. I plan to give her one for Christmas. We can discuss that at a later date."

"Thank you. I look forward to helping you give her a gift she will use and enjoy."

Mr. Dimmick sat silently, studying her. He tapped a pencil on the blotter on his desk. "Mrs. Ward, I'm sorry to have to ask you this as it's a most personal subject, but company policy says I must."

"There's no need, Mr. Dimmick. I know. Yes, I am in the family way. I didn't know when I took the position. My husband had just passed away and I needed a job."

"You don't need to explain. I'm sorry, but company policy doesn't allow for your further employment at this time."

"Yes, sir. I've cleaned out my cubby and left an order for needed items in my department. I want to say, I've enjoyed my time working here and hope you think I was an asset to Townsend and Wyatt."

Mr. Dimmick smiled. "Yes, Mrs. Ward. You've proven to be an exemplary employee. I've placed a letter of recommendation into your file in case you ever want to return or need it to seek work elsewhere. I've enjoyed getting to know you and having you under my supervision."

"Thank you, sir."

He handed her a slip of paper. "Take this to accounting. They will write out your final paycheck. You'll see that I have added two more weeks worth of pay. I hope it helps."

"Thank you, Mr. Dimmick." Pearl rose to leave.

"One more thing, Mrs. Ward. Please tell Miss Miller that I hope she learns to keep hold of the items she purchases in the future." Mr. Dimmick's grin and teasing comment softened the blow of losing her job.

~~~~~

Pearl entered the shop. Will took one look at her and went around the counter, meeting her in the middle of the room. "What's the matter?"

"I'm no longer employed at Townsend and Wyatt."

Will couldn't help it. He pulled her to his chest and wrapped his arms around her. "Oh, honey." That was all he could say, not wanting to reveal he knew of her condition.

She leaned against him for a moment then straightened. "Where's Lillian?"

"Vernon collected her a few minutes ago. He's taking her to supper and then dancing, I think. Lillian was begging to go to the movie house and see what was playing there."

"Are you staying to work? I can fix supper for us." She moved behind the counter, placing the bag she carried on the workbench.

Will wanted to tell her he knew why she no longer had

her job. Wanted to tell her everything would be fine. Wanted to tell her his plan, but also knew he needed to approach the topic gently. That she offered no reason for why she was now unemployed warned him not to start asking a lot of questions.

"Yes, thank you. I would appreciate that."

Pearl turned away and began climbing the stairs. Will looked at the bag she had left behind. He looked in and saw the skeins and cones of the thread she crocheted with. He knew she received a discount on what she purchased at Townsend and Wyatt. She must have bought out all they had, taking a final advantage of it.

While Pearl made them a meal, Will worked and thought about how to bring up the subject and some way to convince her of the correctness of his plan. He'd thought of little else since he'd found out about her condition. He was no closer to a method when she called down that supper was ready than he had been before. He went up the stairs praying for inspiration and that she would be accepting of his suggestion.

Pearl was setting a platter of pork chops on the table that already had potato salad, green beans, and muffins waiting to be eaten. There was a pitcher of cool water, too.

"I didn't make dessert, but there are some cookies in the jar," Pearl said as she sat down across from him.

Will said grace and they filled their plates. She was a good cook, more talented with herbs and spice than Lillian or his mother. He watched as Pearl ate a few bites then began pushing the food around on her plate.

"Pearl, you have to eat." Will laid his fork on the edge of his plate.

"I'm not very hungry." She was looking down at her plate.

"Still, you have to eat," he said softly.

Startled eyes flew their gaze to his. "You know. Lillian

told you. She promised she wouldn't say anything." Pearl jumped up, intending to run from the small kitchen. Will caught her before she escaped, grabbing her shoulders from behind. He pulled her back and put an arm across, pressing her shoulders against him. She stood stiff in front of him.

"Don't blame Lillian. I pressed her, and you know how she is. Little clues just spilled out. I'd been concerned about you for weeks. I finally realized what it was. I didn't say anything, knowing you'd have to say something sometime soon. It's not as if you could keep it secret forever."

Pearl relaxed her stance. "What am I going to do, Will? I've been let go from my job. I can't rely on the lace making to support me. It's too uncertain. I'm not going to be able to keep living here. There's not enough room for Lillian, me, and a baby."

She raised a hand and brushed at her cheek. Will realized she was crying. He turned her around and wrapped his arms around her. He placed his chin on top of her head. "It'll work out. God has a plan. Right now, I want you to eat. You need it, and so does the baby. After, we'll talk about it. Come, sit down. Let's finish the meal. There's nothing that won't wait."

~~~~~

Pearl forced down every bite. Will was right. She needed to eat. Neither one spoke as they finished the meal. Will helped her do the dishes, then took her hand and led her to the davenport in the parlor. They sat facing each other.

"Pearl, do you have a plan as to how to proceed?" Will asked.

Pearl looked at his hand holding hers. "No, not really. I've been saving every penny, but I haven't any idea how long it will last. The wedding dress, I should be able to complete it more quickly now. I thought maybe I could place an advertisement in the newspaper or some publication wealthy people read. I don't know what it would be though."

"Those are good ideas. If you make some larger items, we could display them in the windows. That might help bring in new customers and lead to more commissions." Will squeezed her hand. "I have another idea. One that would bring you more security."

Pearl studied his face. "What?" She watched as he took a deep breath and released it.

"You and I could get married."

"Oh, Will, that's a most generous offer, but you don't need to, and shouldn't, sacrifice your future for me. I'll find some way to manage."

"It's not a sacrifice. I've been drawn to you from the first time I saw you. You have brought something into my life that I didn't even know was missing."

Pearl tilted her head to the side. "I did? What could possibly be missing from your life? You have a successful business, a loving family? What could I bring to it?"

"Peace. You exude peace, Pearl. You know my mother and Lillian. You have to admit, neither one of them are peaceful to be around. That's what you've brought to me. When you are near, there's a calmness, a peace, a relaxation of tension. I love my family dearly, but calm and restful are not adjectives associated with them."

His comment made her smile. He was correct, no one in his family could be considered tranquil. "Wanting some peace in your life isn't a reason to marry."

"No, but if you are attracted to the one who brings that peace, it can be. Pearl, I am very attracted to you."

Pearl was surprised and yet, when she thought about it, she wasn't. Will had always been attentive, showing her every courtesy and respect. The way he treated her on the Fourth of July was more than as a friend. She hadn't wanted to admit he was treating her more like he was courting her than simply being the other chaperone for

Lillian and Vernon. She hadn't wanted to admit that she enjoyed it also. She was still in mourning for Patrick, after all.

"I don't know, Will. It seems like such a drastic thing for you to do. Give up the possibility of finding someone to love by marrying a woman expecting a child."

"Love is more than an emotion. It's an action. An act of the will. If we decide to love the way it is demonstrated in the Bible, then we could have a love grander than anyone who simply falls in love."

"You make it sound so easy. Marriage isn't easy, Will."

"I know it's not. Remember, I've seen my parents be married my entire life."

Pearl gave a weak chuckle. "Still, it's not that simple; the decision to get married." She looked down at her lap. Will squeezed her hand.

"I want you to think about it. Sleep on it. You are tired. It had to be difficult to lose your job. We can talk about it more tomorrow. Just know this, I am not only willing to marry you, I want to. I also want to raise your child as my own. When the time comes, we will tell him or her about Patrick. That's only right, but the child will have Miller as a last name."

Will's willingness to accept her child touched her heart. This wasn't only about her. It was what was best for her child. His not pressing her for an answer tonight demonstrated what she already knew about him— his consideration. He was a good man. A generous, caring man. That made her choice even more difficult.

CHAPTER THIRTEEN

As Pearl lay in bed, she stared at the ceiling. Light from the street lights filtered in through the lace curtains, making intricate patterns on the ceiling.

What was she going to do? Will had offered to shoulder all her difficulties. Solve all her problems. To chase away the fearful demons chasing her. From that viewpoint the choice was simple. Marry him and let him take care of her and the baby.

Looked at from a different angle, was it fair to Will? He'd be taking on a wife, whom he said he was attracted to. She could believe that. Pearl also had to admit she was attracted to him. She hadn't thought that would be possible so soon after Patrick's death.

She had loved Patrick with all her heart. For weeks after his death, Pearl had cried herself to sleep from missing him. During those first days working at Townsend and Wyatt, she'd spent her break times crying in the ladies' retiring room. Each day had gotten easier.

Pearl still missed him terribly, in all ways, but concerns about her future and that of their child overshadowed her grief. She had to make plans and deal with the everyday aspects of life and what was to come. She couldn't focus on what she had lost.

Could she be a wife to Will? A wife in every sense of the word? If she didn't think that was possible, then marriage didn't need to be considered. It wouldn't be fair to Will. He was giving up the possibility of finding his true love. Her being a ready and willing lover was the least she could offer.

Pearl remembered their trip through the Old Mill Waterway at the amusement park. She'd felt his intense desire for her. At the time she denied it, as she'd been confused with her own yearnings. She still loved Patrick.

Now, as Pearl lay in the dark, she had to admit, she was attracted to Will. They fought with her feelings for Patrick. But he was gone, forever. Still, he'd only been gone a few months. If she wasn't expecting Patrick's child, Pearl wouldn't have to consider marrying a man so soon after her husband's passing. She also knew Will would never have mentioned his attraction to her until her year of mourning was over.

Will was a man of character. Not once had he made any move to show his desire for her, to compromise, or encroach on her person. Okay, he'd taken some liberties on the rides by placing his arm around her, but that had been to safeguard her and to help her feel more secure when she was frightened. Pearl could almost see Lillian's eyes rolling at that thought. She grinned in the dark.

Pearl turned on her side. What would Lillian say if she agreed to marry Will? What would his family say? Especially Will's mother.

Mrs. Miller had been so very friendly and helpful when they first met. Then her attitude toward her had changed. Had his mother realized Will's attraction to Pearl and not approved? Pearl's heart sank. If she didn't approve of her son's attraction, then she would object to the marriage.

Could Pearl stand living so close to a disapproving mother-in-law? Would Mrs. Miller take out her enmity on the baby? How would Will deal with conflict between his wife, child, and his mother? For that matter, how would she herself deal with hostility?

Pearl didn't want to come between mother and son. All

she wanted was a secure future for her child. Will was offering that. At least as secure a future as anyone might have. Pearl knew security could be taken away in very short order.

Will had told her to sleep on the decision. Pearl was trying to do that, but the questions kept rolling around in her mind, making her sleep come in fits and starts.

~~~~~

Will rubbed his eyes. He hadn't slept well and Pearl hadn't come downstairs yet this morning. Lillian had bounced down the stairs telling him all about her evening out with Vernon. The conversation hadn't required much input from him, for which Will was grateful.

Glancing at the clock, Will noticed that it was after ten. Pearl still hadn't appeared. There hadn't been footsteps heard overhead either. When Lillian finished with a customer, Will said, "Pearl hasn't come down. Was she awake when you were up there last?"

"No, I peeked into her room, and she was still asleep. I think she had a restless night. The bedclothes were very disturbed, pulled out and nearly falling off the bed. Do you want me to go up and check on her?"

The inquisitive look on his sister's face made him stop the affirmative answer. Since their discussion when he found out about Pearl's condition, they hadn't mentioned anything about it to each other. Will knew Lillian was concerned about Pearl and her future. He didn't think she had any idea that he intended to ask Pearl to marry him. At this point, he didn't want her to know. This was between Pearl and him. Will didn't want Lillian influencing Pearl either way.

"No, I was just wondering. It's not like Pearl not to at least come down and say good morning."

The shop door opened, admitting another customer which took Lillian's focus off him. Will went back to working on the watch he was cleaning.

A few minutes later, he could hear Pearl moving around in the apartment. He hoped she would come down soon. Not that they could have any private discussions with Lillian and customers in the shop. It wasn't like he and Pearl could go upstairs alone to talk. It would have to wait. He would think of something.

Pearl came downstairs carrying a tray with coffee and several pieces of coffeecake. "Good morning. I'm sorry I slept so late. How are you both today?" Though she was smiling, it didn't reach her eyes.

Will studied her. There were dark smudges under her eyes, evidence that she hadn't slept better than he had. Her reasons were most likely different from his. Will simply wanted her to decide to marry him. Her decision was made more difficult because of all the factors involved. He'd spent several hours in the night trying to look at it from her point of view so he could counter any arguments she might raise.

Lillian began her recitation of her evening with Vernon again. That allowed both he and Pearl to simply listen and the atmosphere of tension between them to dissipate.

The rest of the morning felt like any other Saturday with Pearl crocheting in her sewing chair at the end of the workbench. Will working on repairs and waiting on customers. Lillian helped with sales and straightened displays.

Near noon, Lillian went up to make lunch. Will looked at Pearl who was concentrating on her stitches. He gave a wry grin. She was avoiding him even as she sat next to him.

"Pearl?" Will waited until she looked at him. "We need to complete our discussion of last night, but I don't want to do it where Lillian can overhear." He kept his voice low so there was no chance of his sister overhearing.

Pearl gave a slight nod.

"Would you be willing to go for a walk with me, to 'stretch our legs' after we eat? We can go to the park a couple of blocks away. They have benches we can sit on. Lillian can mind the shop."

Again, all he got was a nod.

Will laid a hand on hers. "It'll all work out. Don't fret."

Pearl looked down and pulled her hands from under his and began her stitching again.

~~~~~

Will and Pearl walked the blocks to the park in silence. Will didn't think it boded well for their discussion. Pearl had been nearly silent all morning and during lunch. He noticed Lillian eyeing her friend several times. When he'd suggested that he and Pearl take a stroll to get some fresh air, Lillian had eyed him suspiciously.

They entered the small park and he steered her to a bench under an arbor. When they were seated, Will turned to her. "Pearl, you are so quiet. It's worrying me. Are you all right?"

"I'm expecting a child, have no job, no real means of supporting myself. I'm still grieving my husband, and now face the prospect of marrying mainly to give my child security. I don't want to ruin the life of the dear man who has asked for my hand and is willing to become the father of another man's child. Other than all that, I'm fine."

That she gave him a slight grin brought hope to his heart. "Why do you think our marrying would ruin my life?"

"You deserve to marry someone who you care for deeply, not out of a sense of obligation to a woman you barely know in order to help her out of a difficult situation."

"I helped a woman I didn't know when she fainted in my shop from hunger. I've gotten to know her and for whom I've begun to feel deeply." Will took both her hands in his. "She's brought much joy to my life as well as the peace I mentioned last night. She's talented, hardworking, generous, witty, she can tolerate my sister to the point of actually living with her."

They both chuckled at his comment.

"I like your sister. She's fun."

Will squeezed her hands. "Do you like me?"

"Yes, Will, I do."

"Enough to marry me even though it is not because of love?" he asked. He so wanted to tell her he did want to marry her for love but knew she wouldn't accept it as the truth.

Pearl seemed to search his face with her eyes looking for something. "You said something last night that has stayed in my thoughts ever since. You said that love is an act of the will. That if we commit to each other that we will love as the Bible instructs, then we can have a grand love, grander than if we fell in love. I'm willing, Will, if you are, to try to make a marriage with a goal of that grand love."

Will lifted a hand to her cheek. "It will take both of us working to that goal, but I believe we can accomplish it. I know I will do all in my power to be a good husband and father."

"I will do all in my power to be a good wife and mother to any child we might have."

A tightness Will hadn't known was within him released. Pearl was telling him this would not be a marriage in name only. She would be a wife to him in every sense of the word. He hadn't even been aware of the fear that he might live with this woman he loved and not be able to love her with his body as he did his heart.

Will couldn't stop himself. He leaned in and gave her a gentle kiss, tasting her for the first time. Her lips were soft and sweet. "Thank you."

Pearl's hand was shaking. She tried to hold it steady but was failing miserably. Behind her, Lillian laughed. Looking up at Will, Pearl saw a smile on his face. Cool metal slid onto her ring finger.

"With this ring, I thee wed." Will went on reciting the vows. Pearl was now Mrs. William Miller. It had all happened so quickly.

After their discussion in the park, they'd gone back to the shop. Lillian was busy with a customer. Will had gone straight to the telephone and rung the pastor of their church, arranging for them to meet with him that evening. They had decided to simply get a marriage license and have the man marry them at the parsonage. There would be no fanfare or reception. Because of her status as a recent widow, that would have been unseemly.

Once the shop was empty of customers, they had told Lillian. At first she simply stared, her eyes flitting from one to the other as they stood next to each other. Will held Pearl's hand. It had seemed as if he never let it go unless he needed both hands to do something.

They'd stood watching Lillian for any sort of reaction. Then, in true Lillian fashion, she erupted with excitement, squealing and hugging each of them over and over. Then she sobered. "Have you told anyone else? Have you called Father and Mother? Are you going to? When is the wedding? Am I invited? Can I be the maid of honor? Have you told Mary and Josey? Oh, they will be so excited. Can I tell them if you haven't? They always know everything before I do."

It had taken several minutes to calm her down and begin to explain their plans. Lillian had been disappointed that there wasn't going to be a huge church wedding, but understood, considering the circumstances.

Another customer entered, cutting the discussion short. Several more came keeping all three of them busy. Pearl helped with those wanting lace items. She even took an order for a lace coat.

When they were alone again, Will outlined what he and Pearl had decided on as they had walked back to the shop from the park. They would tell the siblings and their families after church tomorrow with firm promises that no one contact their parents about the decision or the wedding that would be occurring so quickly.

The insistence on not informing the elder Millers bothered Pearl. Why weren't they being told before the ceremony? Everyone seemed concerned over their reaction. Every time she tried to speak with Will about it, he wouldn't meet her eyes and changed the subject. Unsure of herself, Pearl decided not to bring it up until necessary. The couple hadn't informed any of the family as to when they would be returning to St. Joe.

"You may kiss your bride."

The pastor's words brought Pearl out of her reverie. She looked at Will who was smiling down at her. Since the kiss in the park, he'd kissed her several times. Each had been sweet in its own way.

Saturday evening, Will had brought her back to the shop after their meeting with Pastor Phillips. Lillian was upstairs eagerly waiting for Pearl to tell her all the details about their time at the parsonage. Will had kept hold of her hand, not allowing her to leave him.

"Don't let my sister keep you up all night talking. You need your sleep."

"I won't. We'll talk a while. I have to allow her to quiz me some." Pearl smiled.

Will smiled back. "I suppose you do. But, remember, you are sleeping for two and those two mean a lot to me. We have plans for next Thursday, not to mention we have to go to the courthouse for the marriage license on Monday."

"I know. Tomorrow will be an eventful day too, telling

your other sisters and their families. Will they be as excited at Lillian is?"

Will's look gave her pause. He was still smiling but there was a shadow in his eyes. "They will be happy for me, for us. They'll be surprised, maybe even shocked, but we can explain it all to them. I'm sure they will support us. It doesn't matter anyway. It's my life, our lives. Yours, mine, and the baby's. We three are all who truly matter." He grinned. "Plus we have Lillian on our side. There's no stopping that freight train."

"No, there definitely isn't," Pearl giggled.

"I have something I want to give you. No, that's not quite right." He opened a drawer and took out something, hiding it in his hand. He stood close and brought his hand to her bodice and pinned her watch-locket above her left breast.

"I've been wanting to return this to you ever since you sold it to me. I've looked at it often and thought of you. Now, I return it to you since there is no need for you to pay back the loan I made to you. I'll be able to see it often as you will be there for me to look at and think about."

Tears came to Pearl's eyes. "Oh, Will. Thank you."

Will pulled her close. "Well, Mrs. Ward. I must leave you at the base of the stairs. Shall I come collect you and Lillian for worship service tomorrow?" He tipped her chin up, looking down into her face.

Pearl smiled. "I think we can make it there on our own. We have been able to before."

"Okay, but this will be the last time you attend church without me escorting you there."

"I suppose that's true."

Will lowered his head and captured her lips with his for a long moment. "Until tomorrow." He stepped away. "I'll lock the door. Go up and face the interrogation by my sister."

~~~~~

Will looked down into Pearl's face. She was smiling, but a shadow marked her eyes. Was she thinking of Patrick? Remembering their wedding? He knew she was still in the early stages of grief. Patrick had only been gone about four months, and here she was getting married. Will knew she would never have considered his suit if she wasn't expecting Patrick's child. If she hadn't been in desperate circumstances. He wouldn't have pursued her if there hadn't been a baby involved.

Pearl would have gone on working at Townsend and Wyatt and living with Lillian. He would have waited at least until the end of her mourning before he asked to court her, but he would have at some point.

The need to provide for her child was the only reason Pearl would have considered his suit at this time. He hoped there was an underlying attraction to him, at least a little. She seemed to enjoy his company, but that didn't mean she was drawn to him physically. Well, time would tell. Right now, he had a bride to kiss.

Will framed her face with his hands and kissed her with as much of his desire as he could, considering his siblings, their spouses, and their children were gathered around the parlor of the parsonage. As he broke the kiss, someone began clapping. He looked and saw smiles on his sisters' faces. It was gratifying to see Mary's and Josey's eyes telling him of their support. It was something he hadn't been sure of.

When he had taken Pearl by the hand at the picnic when the entire family was gathered in Mary and Clyde's yard after worship, there had been questioning glances. The shocked silence that followed his announcement of their plans for marriage and the date of the wedding, had mouths dropping open. Will had glanced at Pearl whose face was growing red with embarrassment.

"No, well, yes, um. It's just…" Will stammered.

"It's not like that. You know Pearl is a widow. It seems

her late husband, Patrick, left her with a growing gift before he died," Lillian had taken up the explanation gauntlet. Bless her heart. "Pearl was working at Townsend and Wyatt but lost her job due to her condition. Now, she doesn't have a way to support herself, and Will wants to marry her for the sake of her baby, as well as other reasons. I think it's a very romantic thing to do. I'm delighted to soon be able to call Pearl my sister." Her words seemed to break the stunned silence and they were given heartfelt, if reserved, congratulations.

Mary had taken Will aside later. "What are you going to do if the baby is a boy? He would stand to inherit the shop. Neither Father or Mother will stand for that, and Mother will be very vocal about it."

"We'll cross that bridge if we come to it. The baby could be a girl and it won't matter. Pearl will be my wife and I'll be raising the child, boy or girl, as my own. I've told Pearl that."

"Does she know about the shop going to the first boy born?" Mary asked. There was suspicion in her tone.

"No, I didn't tell her. I didn't want it influencing her decision. I knew she wouldn't accept my proposal if she knew. Mary, this is what I want. I tell you this in confidence. Lillian doesn't even know. I'm in love with Pearl. She's everything I've ever wanted in a wife. I was planning on waiting until next year. The baby only sped up my plans." Will stopped talking.

Mary was smiling at him. She patted his cheek. "I'm glad to hear you saying that, but if you think Lillian doesn't know then you don't know her very well. Her little comment, 'as well as other reasons' gave it away."

Will looked at his siblings and their spouses and children. They'd insisted on attending the ceremony, humble as it was. They would be going to Mary and Clyde's home for a simple supper and wedding cake. Josey had insisted on cake. She was nearing her confinement and eating everything she could get her hands on.

~~~~~

Will held Pearl's hand as they walked up the sidewalk to their house. *Their house*, Will thought, *not his*. He was looking forward to the night. At least he hoped it would be a wedding night. He and Pearl hadn't really discussed it. There hadn't been private time since they'd told Lillian. His sister had taken over the planning, organizing everything.

Last evening, his brothers-in-law had helped switch Will's narrow bed at the house for Pearl's double bed in the apartment. Will was glad Lillian had thought of it since it hadn't crossed his mind, which surprised him. The bed was comfortable though it gave Will pause to think Pearl's baby had been conceived in that bed with another man. The next children would be conceived in the same place but with him.

"It was good of Josey's husband to offer to take Lillian back to the shop so we didn't have to go downtown then come back here," Pearl said. "Do you think she'll be okay living there by herself?"

"She'll have to be, unless she wants to move back in with Mother and Father. I can't imagine her doing so. Besides, she might not be living there much longer."

Pearl gave him a questioning look.

"I think she's going to badger Vernon into offering for her hand as soon as she can. He doesn't stand a chance if she sets her mind to have him propose. He might as well just ask and get it over with."

"She's not that bad. She's sweet and funny and…" Pearl screwed her mouth to the side trying to think of the right words.

"Determined, stubborn?" he offered.

"Single-minded."

Will laughed. "She is that."

They'd reached the door and Will unlocked it and swung it open. He bent and scooped Pearl up in his arms.

"Eek!" she squeaked.

"Just following tradition. Carrying you across the threshold." Will set her on her feet but didn't release her. Instead, he held her close and lowered his mouth capturing hers. This kiss included all his desire and the passion he wanted to show her that night. When he broke the kiss, Will looked at her, searching her face for any sign of unease. "Pearl, I know you are still in mourning for Patrick. If you want me to, I'll wait, but know this; I want you to be my wife in all ways. I want to show you how I can worship your body as our vows said. The decision is yours. If you are uneasy about…"

Pearl stopped his words with her fingers. "Shush. I made vows today to be your wife. I loved Patrick. We had a good, passionate marriage. I've missed that. He's gone. I miss him, but you are my husband now. I want you as my husband as you want me as your wife."

Will kissed her then, putting all his longing into it. Pearl returned his desire as she kissed him back.

When they broke apart, breathless, Will took her hand and led her to their bedroom.

~~~~~

Pearl heard the slight clink and knew it had happened again. Her wedding band had fallen off her finger while she did the dishes. They'd known the ring was too big when they got married. Will had planned to re-size it, but the day after the wedding the gems and platinum had arrived for his commission pieces, and he'd begun the work on them. Pearl wasn't going to bother him with the small detail of her ring size.

They'd been married about two weeks and had settled into a routine. Will left for the shop after breakfast. Pearl would do her housework and, depending on how long it took, she would go to the shop in the late morning or Will would come home for lunch. They would go back to the shop, and she would crochet and help with customers in the afternoon.

Often they stayed to eat supper with Lillian as she was a little low being alone all evening. Often on those days Vernon would join them, leaving when they did early in the evening. It wouldn't do for him to stay with Lillian alone in the apartment.

With the added hours Pearl could devote to crocheting, the wedding gown was ready to be fitted. She was going to the Clarys' as soon as her chores were done. When the fitting was complete, she'd go to the shop. Rather than explain the change in her circumstances, Pearl arranged for the fitting to be on Saturday.

Pearl fished the ring out of the dishwater and placed it on the windowsill. She finished washing the dishes, setting them in a rack to dry. Drying her hands, she rubbed Pond's Vanishing Cream into them and took off her apron.

Making sure her attire and hairstyle were in order, Pearl gathered her handbag and bag holding the folded crochet gown. She hurried out of the house to the trolley stop and soon arrived at the Clarys'.

Both Mrs. Clary and Daisy were excited with the gown. The only thing left was the border around the hem which Pearl promised to have done within two weeks.

As she left the yard, Mr. Guy Clary fell into step beside her. Pearl picked up her pace.

"I know all about you, Mrs. Ward, and I have a proposition for you. I know you are living with that jeweler. I'm sure he cannot support you as I can. I will set you up in a house of your own. You won't have to slave making lace for the wealthy. You can live like one. All you'll have to do is entertain me a few evenings a week. The rest of your time will be yours to do with as you please. All it would take is a bit of discretion on your part to keep our set up a secret. That wouldn't be too difficult, now would it?"

Pearl was shocked speechless. She'd known he was interested in her but had never considered that he would offer to make her his mistress. Not knowing what to say, she said nothing. She kept walking as fast as she could.

He took her left hand and lifted it to his lips. With his eyes locked onto hers, he kissed her ring finger. "Such a pretty little hand with no ring on it. Now that you've crossed from grieving widow to kept woman, there won't be a ring on this ever again. What does it matter who the man is who pays the bills? I can make your future more lavish than you could ever imagine."

Pearl snatched her hand away. "I'll pardon your rudeness since the announcement hasn't been made. I am now Mrs. William Miller. Please refrain from making such insulting comments and offers in the future."

Mr. Clary laughed. "You expect me to believe a jeweler would not present his wife with a wedding ring? That goes beyond comprehension. No, Mrs. Ward, I don't believe you have married the jeweler, but do not worry. The offer stands, at least for a while. Who knows when another comely young woman will catch my eye. I'll let you think on my generous offer and inquire for your reply another day."

Fortunately, the trolley was just coming to a halt at the stop and she was able to climb on, drop her coins in, and find a seat on the street side of the car. She glanced out the window and saw a smirk on Guy Clary's face. He'd crossed the street and was staring at her. Pearl faced forward, not looking at him. The driver rang the bell and the trolley began its journey along its route.

Instead of going to the shop, Pearl went home. There was no way she could hide her upset from Will. At least, not right away. She telephoned the shop letting them know she was not coming to the shop until later. Pearl pleaded fatigue and several other chores needing to be done.

With shaking hands, she picked up her wedding ring and slid it on her finger.

CHAPTER FOURTEEN

Pearl stood next to Will on the platform of the train station. Lillian fluttered between their sisters and nieces and nephews. Mary's husband, Clyde, and Josey's husband, Fred, stood nearby. They'd all come to greet the elder Millers as they arrived home from their time in Hot Springs, Arkansas.

Pearl wrung her hands until Will took hold of one, giving it a squeeze. "It'll be okay. They both like you. They'll be surprised, yes, but will be happy for us."

Pearl wasn't so sure. Keeping Will's parents in the dark about their marriage had never been a good idea in her mind. Will had insisted on keeping it a secret until they came home. Pearl had acquiesced to his wishes. At least they wouldn't make a scene on the platform when they were told. Or would they? Pearl didn't know them well enough to predict.

A whistle sounded in the distance. The children cheered, anxious for Gramma and Grampa to return. They all gathered at the end of the platform allowing other families to get ready to board or greet returning family members. Pearl stepped slightly behind Will.

The locomotive belching black smoke slowed as it moved past. The train stopped with the passenger cars next to the platform. Smoke obscured the view and caused them to close their eyes and cover mouths and noses until the breeze blew it away.

"Grampa," yelled a young voice as Mr. Miller descended the steps and turned to help Mrs. Miller down. Pearl thought he looked much stronger than he had when they left in early July. Nearly two months resting and taking the waters in Hot Springs seemed to have been a benefit.

Will stayed back, holding Pearl's hand as his sisters and their families greeted his parents. The children were excited and jumping around.

"That will be our little one in a few years. My parents dote on their grandchildren."

Pearl hoped that would be true.

It wasn't long before Will and Pearl became the focus of intense looks from the elder Miller couple. Someone must have told about the marriage. Such a secret was hard for little children to hold inside. Pearl stood a little taller and leaned slightly closer to Will. He squeezed her hand again as Matthew and Luella walked over.

"I understand congratulations are in order," Matthew said, his tone making it evident he wasn't pleased to have been left out of the loop.

"Thank you, Father. We are quite happy." Will dropped Pearl's hand and placed his arm around her shoulders.

"Here is not the place or time to speak of the details. We have travelled long and both of us are weary. Mary says she has invited everyone for supper tonight. We will speak of this then. Now, Will, kiss your mother hello. I must supervise the baggage." Matthew walked away without greeting Pearl. Her heart sank.

Will did as instructed. "Welcome home, Mother." He kissed her cheek. "We have missed you both. The shop isn't the same without you coming in regularly."

"It seems you found someone else to keep you company." Luella turned to Pearl. "Hello, Pearl. You are looking well."

"Thank you. Welcome home." Pearl didn't call Will's mother by name. Mrs. Miller didn't seem right, but she hadn't been given leave to use her first name. Nor would she call her Mother unless there was more acceptance of Pearl's relationship with Will and she was asked.

Will moved to help with the luggage and Lillian came to take his place beside Pearl. "Mother, you won't believe how beautiful the wedding gown Pearl has made is. I'm sure she'll be getting many more commissions once it's seen at the Clary wedding."

"I'm sure it is lovely. You have a real talent making lace, Pearl. I look forward to seeing it."

Pearl tried to determine if the words were sincere. From the flat tone she couldn't tell.

The luggage had all been collected and placed in the new motorcars of Clyde and Fred. They and their families would take the couple home to rest before the families gathered for supper at Mary and Clyde's home. That left Lillian, Will, and Pearl to walk back to the shop.

"Well, that went as well as could be expected," Lillian said as they crossed the street. "Father let it be known he's not pleased about not being told, and Mother was at least cordial. It's a promising start. They will get over the hurt of not being able to attend the wedding soon. At least you won't have to tell them about the baby. I'm sure Mary or Josey will let that be known before we get there this evening. You know, I could contact Vernon and have him join us at Mary's tonight. That would stop any harsh words."

"Lillian," Will admonished. "You aren't making this better, but I thank you for your support."

"I'm only trying to help." Dejected, Lillian kicked a stone into the street.

"And I love you for it," Pearl said. "We knew this would come as a shock. They must feel rather betrayed by their children. Especially Will."

"I didn't mean to betray them," Will said.

"You didn't, Will. You did what you wanted and what you felt called to do. You are happy together and that's more important than what Father and Mother think. You have to live your lives as you want, not how they want you to live."

"True," Will said. "But it doesn't make me feel any better about hurting their feelings."

Pearl squeezed his hand, offering what comfort she could.

~~~~~

They were sitting in Clyde Bethel's private office in his home. Matthew sat behind the desk with Luella sitting in a chair he'd placed beside him. The other two chairs held Pearl and Will. The door was closed giving them privacy.

"Was there some reason you failed to inform your mother and me about your marriage, even after the fact? Are you ashamed of your actions?"

"No, of course not. We are very happy. At least, I am." Will glanced at Pearl. She seemed to be trying to fade into invisibility. Her hands were in her lap clenched so tight the knuckles were white. He was regretting not writing his parents once the wedding was over. Not only were his parents angry with him, Pearl was suffering from his choice.

The excuses that flew through his mind were just that. Excuses. It wouldn't have taken very long to write a letter expressing his joy that she had accepted his proposal. Explaining why he didn't honor her year of mourning was going to open another can of worms. It would embarrass Pearl even more.

Will cleared his throat. The things he needed to say might explain the haste. Giving an explanation as to why he hadn't written would sound rather hollow, but at the time, he'd thought they were valid.

"I know our marriage seems ill-timed. Pearl was only

four months into her mourning. She was working at Townsend and Wyatt and her lace was selling well. She and Lillian were getting along famously living together. I had noted some, um, issues concerning her health, however.

"I pressed Lillian on the subject and, you know how she is, she can't keep her mouth closed on a secret." He glanced at Pearl. She was looking at her lap, but her cheeks were red. "I pressed enough and found out that Pearl was in a delicate condition. A legacy from her husband."

"So you asked her to marry you?" Luella asked, disapproval thick in the words.

"No, I knew she would not have agreed. I waited until she was let go from her job." As soon as the words left his mouth, Will realized how they sounded. Both his wife's and mother's gasps told him they heard the implication in them also. "No, it wasn't like that. I wasn't trying to force Pearl to marry me. Actually, it took me several days to work out a solution to her dilemma after I figured it out." That didn't sound right either. He glanced at his father and then away, not liking the disapproval on the face of the man he respected above all others.

Will took a deep breath and started again. "Mother, you knew I was attracted to Pearl. We spoke of it before you left for Hot Springs. Even then, I was wanting to court Pearl but knew it was too soon. My thought was to continue as her friend until after her mourning was over. I'd ask if I could court her at that time. Not only was that proper, but it would give Pearl the opportunity to become attracted to me as I am to her. My respect for her would not have allowed me to reveal my feelings before that time.

"Then, I found out about her condition. I knew she would lose her job and be back in the same situation she was when we met." When his mother began to interrupt, Will put up his hand to stop her. "No, Mother, my feelings are not one of rescuing a damsel in distress. When I realized my feelings toward Pearl, she was working and supporting herself. However, I didn't want her or the baby to suffer and be put in danger because she was unable to support herself."

Will glanced at Pearl again. He wished she would look up at him. He needed to see her eyes to know if she was feeling like he'd manipulated her.

"When I suggested to Pearl that we marry, she refused." He smiled a little at the memory. "It took quite a bit of persuading to get her to agree. She didn't want to burden me with her problems. Tie me to her for a lifetime. I finally was able to convince her that she and her child were not a burden but a blessing who would add immeasurably to my life. She has, and I look forward to the coming addition who will bless us even more."

"What if the baby is a boy, Will?" His father brought the elephant in the room into view. From the corner of his eye, he saw Pearl look up at him. Another thing he should have told her about earlier. This time he'd kept his wife in the dark.

"Pearl doesn't know about that aspect. I've decided that this child will be mine and will be raised as mine in all ways. If it is a boy, and he wants it, the shop will go to him as my first born son just as it has always been."

Pearl gasped. "Oh, Will. You should have told me."

He turned to her in his chair and took her hands. "That's why I didn't. You would not have married me if you knew the tradition. If the baby is a boy, and he wants to be a jeweler, then he will get the shop. If he doesn't, we'll work out an inheritance for him and pass the shop to the next son, if he wants it. It is a tradition, not a law."

Both his parents gasped.

Will turned to face them. "I know to you that is heresy. For generations, the shop has passed to the first son. Grandfather told me about it many times as I was growing up. He also told me how his father gave him, the second son, enough money, an inheritance, to get out of Bavaria so he wouldn't have to fight in the war. I'm doing the same. Planning to give each of our children an inheritance. It's one reason why I'm hoping for more commission work."

Will sighed. Now the next, and he hoped final, issue needing to be addressed. Why he didn't write and tell his parents of the marriage. He faced his parents sitting across the desk from him.

"I realize now, that my reasons for not writing were flimsy at best. Cowardly at worst. I knew you would be upset with our marriage, even though it has made me extremely happy. I rationalized that with this large commission I didn't have time to write an adequate letter explaining everything.

"This commission may bring other commission work. It may establish me as a master jewelry craftsman, allowing me to focus more on creating rather than repairing."

"You think you are too good to repair watches?" Matthew asked stiffly.

"No, of course not. Repairing watches gives me, us, a fine living. It has for years. It is a noble trade and one I enjoy." Will grinned. "Remember the watch the three-year-old boy got a hold of. While you were gone, his father picked up the watch that was now working. He was overjoyed that he could not tell it had ever been damaged. You taught me how to do such fine repair work.

"I want to take the skills you taught me, that Grandfather taught me, and use them to create beautiful pieces of jewelry as well as repair watches and sell what others create.

"I used that desire, and the opportunity for such a large important commission that came at the same time as Pearl's and my marriage, to put off writing to tell you of the great change in my life. I rationalized that I was too busy to write. It was cowardly of me and wrong. It was not how I was raised: to be open and honest in all my dealings. That includes those with family. I am sorry I did not trust that, in your love for me, you would support my choices."

Pearl squeezed his hand. He looked at her. She smiled and squeezed his hand again. Though they'd never said the words, Will could feel her love for him. He hoped that was what she was trying to convey. At the least, she was showing her support and acceptance of his explanations.

"Will," his father said, "though I dislike how you handled all of this." He waved his hands in an encompassing motion. "I'm proud you have owned your errors. Whether the choices you've made recently will bring you and Pearl happiness remains to be seen. You've made a covenant before God and will need to keep that in mind when things get rough in your marriage. We—" he indicated Luella and himself, "will support you. You are an adult and have made your choices. Time will tell if they will were the correct ones."

His father's face showed acceptance. His mother's still held disapproval. Will hoped she would come around and give Pearl the support he knew she needed.

~~~~~

Pearl watched her steps as they walked from the trolley stop toward their home. Several concerns warred within her heart. Will had made choices that estranged him from his parents whom he was very close to. He had omitted telling her about the legacy of the shop. He had deeper feelings for her than he'd let on. The burden of all those weighed heavy on her heart.

She glanced at Will. His countenance was somber. She could tell he felt guilty. Maybe he should, since his choices were what had brought them to this point. A verse from Romans came to mind. *There is no condemnation in Christ.* If there was none in Him, then she should not condemn Will either.

Pearl moved her point of view from herself to him. He loved his parents. He knew their way of thinking. They were very old school. Matthew had been raised on traditions that went back generations. Her child threatened that tradition. She could pray the baby would be a girl, but she figured that had been decided a long time ago, and God probably wouldn't change that at this late date.

Will's declaration of his feelings for her had been surprising. She'd known he was attracted to her, liked her, enjoyed her company. Pearl hadn't realized the depth of his feelings. Though he hadn't used the word, it had seemed as if he was declaring he loved her.

Pearl mulled over how she felt. Were her feelings as strong for Will as his seemed to be for her? She didn't think so. Patrick still held a vast portion of her heart. He always would. She still missed him daily. Her grief was constant but wasn't all consuming as it had been for weeks after he died.

Will took her arm as they stepped off the curb to cross the street. He was occupying more of her heart each day. He treated her so well. Took care to see to her safety and comfort. He had ever since they'd met.

Even before he knew of her condition, Will had always done small things to demonstrate his thoughtfulness. Adding the sewing chair to the work area. Rearranging the space so it wouldn't be as crowded with the three of them all back there.

Recently he'd had more electric lights installed. Will claimed it was so he could see to work better. Pearl realized most of it illuminated the place where she sat.

They'd agreed before they married that they would live as the Bible instructed a marriage to be. The husband was to love his wife sacrificially, the way Christ loved his bride. Will was doing that. He was doing what he could to lift her up, to help her to bring out the best in herself. To help her feel loved, worthwhile, and respected. By doing so, it made the choice to accept his leadership in their home easy. That was a much higher, harder responsibility than her duty to submit. Will was fulfilling that responsibility.

Was he perfect? She looked down and grinned. No, far from it. His mistakes brought out today proved that. He also tended to leave his dirty socks under the bed, and he'd forgotten to resize her wedding ring. But those were small issues. He was very busy working at the shop and creating the pieces of the commission. The ring was a small thing that could be done once the project was complete.

Will placed his hand on Pearl's back, guiding her to precede him up the walk to the house. They'd barely spoken to one another as they journeyed home, both lost in their own thoughts. The silence continued as they got ready for bed.

Pearl lay on her back next to Will as the last of the summer evening faded into darkness. She remembered Luella's face as they said their goodbyes. Pearl wasn't optimistic that her mother-in-law would welcome her into the family. All she could do was be as cooperative and friendly as she could.

Pearl remembered how both her own mother and Patrick's had pushed to be a large part of the newlywed's lives. It had gotten so bad they had moved from Ohio to Missouri. And both of the mothers had approved of their marriage. Will's mother didn't. That was obvious.

Pearl decided Will would never hear her complain about how Luella, as Matthew had instructed her to be called, treated her. He felt bad enough about how he'd handled the situation and the hurt he had caused both his parents. Pearl wouldn't become more of a wedge between mother and son than she already was.

~~~~~

"I never did it that way."

Pearl fought to keep from rolling her eyes. It had to be about the millionth time she'd heard Luella say that same phrase. And it was only the second Wednesday after the elder Millers had returned from their trip.

Luella had shown up early the first Monday morning shortly after Will left for the shop. She'd claimed to want to spend time with Pearl getting to know her. Instead, it had become a daily few hours of critical statements.

Pearl didn't use the correct laundry soap. She didn't fold socks the way Will was used to. Shouldn't the eggs be kept in a bowl in the icebox rather than a box? Surely that wasn't enough milk to get them through until the milkman came again in two days. Luella always dusted on Wednesday, not Tuesday. The peaches should be sliced thinner for the pie. That's not the way I do it.

Pearl learned quickly not to reply or try to defend her method. Her views were neither accepted or appreciated. She simply kept silent and plugged away at her tasks. As soon as possible, Pearl would finish her chores and inform Luella she was needed at the shop. Then, she would escape for a few hours of peace before Will's mother made her daily trek to check in with her son and daughter at the family business. That Pearl was normally there didn't impact Luella. She was sweet, kind, and feigned interest in Pearl's conversation or work.

Pearl never mentioned Will's mother's attitude or words to him. She'd made the vow to herself that she would not criticize her mother-in-law. She wondered how long it would take before her frustration with how she was being treated turned to anger and then to an explosion the likes of which St. Joseph had never seen before. Pearl turned her head slightly so Luella couldn't see her face and grinned wickedly. Not that she wanted that to happen, but the thought of the shock on Luella's face just might be worth it. Then again, nothing would be gained, and Will would find out and be placed in the middle between his wife and mother.

"Luella," Pearl said as she untied her apron. "I'm sorry to cut our visit short, but I am delivering the lace wedding gown to the Clary's this morning. From there I will need to come right back and fix Will's lunch. He comes home for lunch every Wednesday, you know. I need to change and be on my way. I'm sure you understand." She glanced at the clock. "Let me see you out. The trolley will be along shortly if you don't want to walk the entire way home."

Luella never had chance to say a word as Pearl escorted her to the front door, closing it as soon as the woman stepped past the threshold. Pearl breathed a sigh of relief and went to change. Now, she just hoped Guy Clary wouldn't be around.

CHAPTER FIFTEEN

Pearl couldn't believe her luck. The obnoxious son of the house hadn't been in evidence either before or after she met with Mrs. Clary and Daisy. Not only was Pearl's lace over-gown complete, but the designer and creator of the silk wedding gown was there so Daisy could finally wear her wedding gown to see if any final alterations were needed.

Daisy looked lovely and would make a beautiful bride. She was so very excited. It would be one of the highlights of the fall season. September was a superb time for a wedding as the humidity of summer was past and yet the days were warm.

Pearl hung her handbag in the closet, giving it a pat. She would deposit the check Mrs. Clary had given her in the bank when she accompanied Will back to the shop after they ate lunch. She was excited to show him the amount. Mrs. Clary had added an additional amount as a 'tip' for a job well done. She had also promised to give Pearl a photograph of Daisy wearing the gown so it could be used as a reference for the 'absolutely gorgeous' gown she had made for her beloved daughter.

Pearl was in the kitchen preparing lunch when she heard the front door open. "I'm in here, Will," she called. "I'm so excited. Mrs. Clary and Daisy loved the dress. She looked so lovely in it." She turned around to face him and stepped back with a gasp.

Will wasn't standing in the doorway to the hall. It was Guy Clary. Dressed in an off-white linen suit complete with vest and blue four-in-hand tie, he smiled. "I'm glad to know my mother and sister liked the gown. Now that your business with my family is completed, there can't be any reason why you can't move from the protection of the watch repairman to mine. I can certainly set you up in a much better house than this." He looked around with a sneer.

"How dare you come into my home without knocking. Just who do you think you are?" Pearl was shocked at the rudeness of the man.

"Come on, Mrs. Ward, Pearl. Such a lovely name. A gem of a name and one I'll be whispering as I make love to you tonight." He stepped forward, his arms lifting to embrace her.

Pearl stepped back, bumping into the counter. She whirled around, grabbing the knife she'd been using and held it up. "Step back, Mr. Clary."

Instead of being terrified, she was mad. Furious. He'd not taken her refusals as fact, even after she told him she was remarried. Her frustration at being at the mercy of her mother-in-law's treatment added to the anger she felt toward Guy Clary.

"I'd step back if I were you, Mr. Clary. I will tell you one more time. I have made it clear on a number of occasions that I am not interested in being anything of yours. I told you I have remarried and am now Mrs. Miller. I want you to leave now and not return or ever come into my presence again. I've kept my peace about your behavior since I don't want to come between mother and son, but I will if you ever approach me for even a hello. Now get out."

"You heard my wife, Mr. Clary." Will's cold steel hard voice had Pearl looking past her tormentor and Guy turning around. Will stood in the doorway looking angrier and more dangerous than she'd ever seen him before.

"I believe my wife," Will emphasized the word, "asked you to leave. I suggest you do as she requested. At the moment I'm holding my temper in check. If you want to walk away, don't say anything, as a single word might cause me to lose control and pound you into the floor."

Guy looked Will up and down. "You can't blame me for the mistake in not realizing she was married. She wears no ring. A jeweler whose wife doesn't wear a wedding ring?" He lifted an eyebrow in question.

"Her words should be good enough for you. I heard her say she's told you before of her marital status. You insult her by your actions and words and also by your considering her a liar. Get out now, before I change my intent to allow you to leave under your own power, beat you senseless for your lack of respect and insults, and toss you out into the street like the garbage you are." Will stepped forward, lifting his fists.

"My pardon, Mrs. Miller." The sneer in his words belied their sincerity. Guy tried to brush passed Will who had had enough of the rake's insinuations toward his wife.

Will grabbed him by his blue tie and hauled his face close. "You better heed my words and change your attitude before I change my mind about allowing you to leave unscathed." Will kept hold of Guy's tie and dragged him out the front door. Letting the man go at the edge of the porch, Will lifted his foot and landed a swift kick to the seat of Guy's pants, sending him sprawling across the lawn. When he rose and faced Will the front of his suit was stained green from the grass.

Will looked down at Guy from the porch. "I wonder how you are going to explain those grass stains to your mother. She's quite a fan of my wife and her talents. So is your sister. How do you suppose they would react to how you've been treating her?"

Guy paled a little, turned on his heel, and stalked away,

not looking back.

Will found Pearl still standing in the kitchen. The knife dropped to the floor and Pearl covered her face with shaking hands. Then, she was embraced against Will's chest.

"Are you all right?" Will pressed her to him, and she wrapped her arms around his waist.

"I'll be fine in a few minutes. Just let me stay here. Hold me. I'll quit shaking in a moment, I'm sure."

Once she'd calmed, Will leaned back so he could see her face. "Why didn't you tell me he had been bothering you?"

"Mrs. Clary paid me today when I delivered the dress. I thought that was the end of it."

"He's been doing this all the while you've been going there, hasn't he?"

Pearl searched Will's face. She could tell he was angry but couldn't tell if it was at her or Guy. "Yes, I thought he'd just give up once the gown was done."

"That sort of man doesn't give up unless someone lets him know there will be dire consequences to their actions."

"I figured that out. That's why I had the knife. Will, I'm sorry. I should have told you. If he comes back I'll let you know immediately."

"Be sure you do," Will said with conviction, then he chuckled and kissed the top of her head. "You certainly were ferocious with that huge knife. I'm sure you could have done quite a bit of damage."

Pearl looked down at the knife on the floor. The paring knife's blade was only about three inches long. "Even a knife as small as that could have been deadly with the anger I had toward him at that moment. He's been a thorn in my side ever since the first day I met him. The stupid man wouldn't take no for an answer even when I told him I was married."

Will tipped her chin up with his finger. "Why aren't you wearing your wedding ring?"

"It's too large and keeps falling off. I'm afraid I'll lose it."

"I failed you, Pearl. I'm sorry. I knew the ring was too large when we married. I promised to correct the size and forgot to do so. I'm sorry. You should have mentioned it."

"You've been so busy with your commission pieces. They are much more important than my wedding ring."

Will kissed her. "No, sweetheart. You are much more important than the commission. I'll work on the ring this afternoon. By supper you'll have the ring on your finger with no fear it will be lost."

"Will, it's not important. It can wait."

"No, you are the most important person in my life and a priority over everything else. I'm resizing your ring today."

Rather than telling him how much she appreciated his insistence, she pulled his mouth to hers and showed him.

~~~~~

Pearl lay snuggled against Will and held up her left hand. Not only had he resized her wedding ring, but he had given her an engagement ring. Both were yellow gold. The wedding ring was a plain wide 18 karat band. The engagement ring had a peridot stone surrounded by small pearls. He'd chosen the pale green stone to represent the month when they married. The pearls were an obvious choice.

"I know we didn't truly have a betrothal, but I want you to have a ring." He'd placed the rings on her finger, kissed her hand, then her mouth.

Pearl had shown her appreciation in the way most meaningful to men. Now, they lay together in the semi-darkness, a candle burning on the bedside table.

Something fluttered across Pearl's low abdomen. She stilled, waiting. There it was again.

"Will."

He gave her forehead a sleepy kiss. "What?"

"I felt it."

"Felt what?"

"The baby. I just felt it."

He jerked away, letting her head drop onto the pillow. "You what? Is it okay. Do I need to call a doctor?"

Pearl laughed. "No, silly. It's just getting big enough to where I can feel it."

"Can I feel it?"

"You can try but I doubt you will be able to yet. Wait a few weeks and maybe you'll even be able to see it. I'll be fatter then."

He lay down facing her and stroked her hair that streamed over her shoulders. "Not fatter, just more beautiful."

A yawn stretched Pearl's jaw. "I'm sorry. I'm just so tired."

"You should sleep in tomorrow. I can get breakfast for myself."

"I'll be fine. It's just been a long day." There was no way she was going to be still in bed when Luella came in the morning.

"Do I need to give you an order?" Will used a false authoritative tone.

"No, if I'm too tired I'll stay home and rest or maybe come home early and take a nap. I don't want to miss making you breakfast. It's one of the parts of the day I like best."

"What, looking at the back of the newspaper I'm reading?"

"No, just making sure my husband starts the day off with a good meal."

He kissed her nose. "It's one of my favorite parts of the day too, but to tell the truth, I like the nights better."

Pearl gave his arm a playful slap. "You would."

"I'm going home to celebrate with my wife. I'll find out if she wants to go out to supper. If she does, I'll telephone and also call to see if Vernon would like to tag along," Will told Lillian as he put the morning's proceeds in a leather bag. He was going to deposit this as soon as he locked the shop. There was no way he was going to risk leaving this amount in the shop safe. The necklace, earrings, bracelet, and tiara were complete. Mr. Norbury had come to get them and brought a check for the balance due.

"I think we should close the shop for the rest of the day." Lillian flipped through the signs they placed in the frame on the door giving notice of special hours or closings. "We've been working very hard and deserve an afternoon off, I say."

"It's not afternoon yet, only late morning." Will grinned. "But I think your idea is spot on. Let's get these things put in the safe." He waved a hand at the display cases. "I'll do the windows."

It didn't take long to clear all the jewelry and place it in the safe. It was something they did every day. Lillian left the shop with Will since she wanted to do some shopping and was headed to Townsend and Wyatt. She often came back saying she'd seen Mr. Dimmick and several times 'accidentally' dropped her purchase near where he was standing.

Will rode the trolley home thinking what he wanted to use the money he'd earned on the commission for. He had an idea, but wanted to discuss it with Pearl. It was good to know he could talk over ideas and ask her opinion on things as he thought about decisions needing to be made.

As he entered the house he heard his mother's voice. What she was saying made him frown. He tiptoed down the hall to listen some more before he interrupted her.

"I've told you before, Pearl, you need to pull the sheets toward you as you iron them, not away. I don't understand why you can't remember that. You can't seem to do anything correctly."

Will listened for Pearl's response. There was only silence.

His mother made the grunt she always had that indicated her disapproval of something her children did. "I can't imagine how you'll manage when you have that baby to take care of."

Deciding he'd heard enough and not wanting Pearl to suffer more indignation, Will stepped into the kitchen. Pearl had her back to him as she stood at the ironing board set up near the stove, her flat irons lined up on the top, heating. His mother was sitting at the end of the kitchen table as if she was holding court.

"I do believe Pearl will manage very well when the baby comes. She certainly has managed to make this house a pleasant home in the short time she's been my wife. I'll be pleased if you would refrain from criticizing her. Not everyone does things using the same methods. So long as the job gets done, what difference does it make?"

Pearl spun around, her shock that he was home evident on her face. She looked from him to his mother and back. "Will, what are you doing home? Is anything wrong?"

"There wasn't until I got home. Mr. Norbury picked up the commission set, and Lillian and I decided to take the rest of the day off to celebrate. She's out shopping, and I came home to spend the rest of the day with my wife. Unfortunately, my mother seems to be giving unwanted critiques of my wife's capabilities as a housewife."

Pearl, white-faced, and who he could see was near tears, came over. He wanted to pull her into an embrace, but she murmured, "Excuse me, please." He allowed her to pass him and watched as she went into their bedroom, closing the door with a soft snick.

He advanced two steps into the kitchen and speared

his mother with an angry look. "What is the matter with you? What in the world gave you the impression you needed, and had the right, to come into my home and criticize my wife?"

Will kept his voice low, under tight control. He was furious. He'd noticed Pearl's mood slide from happy and content to despondent and nervous lately. He'd attributed it to her condition. "Have you been doing this since you and Father got home?"

Luella stood. "I'm simply giving her the benefit of my years of experience."

"Did Grandmother give you the benefit of her experience when you and Father married?"

"No, of course not. I knew how to maintain a home when I married. Pearl is so young."

"Pearl is older than you were when you had Mary." Will gritted his teeth. "Age and experience aside, what gives you the right to come into my home and hurt my wife with your cruel words and attitude?"

"I'm your mother."

"Duly noted. My question stands?"

"I only want the best for you."

"And the best is you being cruel and critical to my wife, behind my back."

"You're my son. I love you. Of course I want to make sure you have a properly run home."

"My home is properly run. If it was not, that still wouldn't be any of your business. It would be between Pearl and me to figure and work out."

"But—"

Will raised a hand, stopping her from continuing to defend her actions. "I'm an adult, Mother, not a child who doesn't know how to get on. I have a wife now, one I love. I will not tolerate you treating her in anything but a loving manner.

"Today, I came home to celebrate a very successful

elevation in my career. One I'm very proud of and would hope you and Father will be also. It very well may bring more custom work which will lead to even more prosperity than we've previously enjoyed. I wanted to celebrate that success with the woman I love. Instead, I find my mother butting into my marriage in ways that are mean and spiteful.

"I am not only dismayed that you think you have the right to be so cruel in the name of loving me but appalled that you would do so behind my back. You've treated Pearl well, if not warmly, when we are all at the shop. Then, when I am not around, you've been hateful and critical, haven't you?"

"I supposed she's been complaining to you."

"No, she hasn't said a word, but now I know why she's been less happy and more nervous than when we first married. I've been concerned about her. I thought it was due to her condition, but now I know it's because you've been treating her so poorly."

Will held up his hand when she would have spoken.

"No. I don't want to hear another word. I have several for you, however. With as much as I want to see if the pieces of jewelry I made, and which Mr. Norbury thought were so good, will bring me more success here in St. Joe, I will take my wife and child and move away. Pearl is the woman I love and will be spending the rest of my life with. I will not stay in a town where my mother will be undermining my marriage and disrespecting me.

"I love you, Mother, but I will not allow my wife to be treated as you have been doing. I ask you to leave my home and not return until you are ready to beg forgiveness from Pearl and to treat her with the respect and support she deserves. I also ask that you limit your visits to the shop to when you know Pearl will not be there. I will not subject her to you and your vitriol."

"You would do that to me, your mother?"

"Pearl is my wife. She is the woman I love. For those two aspects alone you should be loving and supportive of her. Until you can do so, you are not welcome in my home. Please see yourself out. My wife needs to know I love her and will protect her from the evil that has been infecting her life and mine."

Will turned his back to his mother and walked from the kitchen.

~~~~~

Will entered the bedroom and closed the door. There was no way he was going to allow his mother to see or hear them. Pearl was lying on the bed, weeping. His mother had done this to Pearl. The thought made his stomach turn.

He'd come home ready to celebrate the success of the commission pieces. Had planned to discuss the possibility of purchasing a motorcar with what he'd earned. He was going to take Pearl and Lillian out to supper in honor of his success. Instead, he needed to comfort his wife who had been suffering abuse from his mother.

He went over and sat beside her, then changing his mind, lay down, and gathered her to him. "Pearl, why didn't you tell me what she was doing? I would have put a stop to it long before now."

"I didn't want to be a wedge between you and her."

"So you let her abuse you with her words and attitude."

"It was a small price to pay to help you and your parents reconcile. I know they were hurt by our marriage. I wanted to do what I could to help them get over it and put it behind us all."

Will tipped her chin up so he could see her face. "Was it working?"

Pearl bit her lip. "I don't think so."

He kissed her forehead. He hugged her. "Today was such a good day. I wanted to share it with you. Lillian and

I closed the shop. She is going shopping, and we all were going to meet for a celebratory supper. I was so happy. Then, I come home to find that my mother has been abusing my wife, the woman I love more than life itself, ever since she and Father came back to St. Joe. Definitely put a damper on my day."

Pearl had jerked back and was looking at him in surprise.

"What?" Will asked in confusion.

"You love me?"

He smiled softly. "Yes, I love you. More than life itself." He repeated the words that had come so naturally only moments before.

"Oh, Will."

"You don't have to say anything. I know you are still mourning Patrick. I only hope you have some affection toward me and maybe it will someday be more.

"Please, Pearl, please, don't let how my mother has been treating you get in the way of our relationship. I told her she was not welcome in our home until she could apologize to you and accept you as my wife. I will not have you disrespected by anyone, especially a family member, even if she is my mother. I also told her not to come to the shop when you are there. I won't have her around you to upset you. It isn't good for you or the baby."

"I can stay home."

"No, I love having you there. I know, once the baby comes, you won't be able to come as often. Until then, I want you there as much as you can be. I love having you with me. Lillian loves to have you there, also."

"I don't want to come between you and your mother and father."

"You aren't. She's the one who brought this on herself. I told her one more thing. It might be what will cause her to truly rethink her actions. If she doesn't change her attitude, I will do it."

Pearl studied his face, drawing her eyebrows together with concern.

"If she can't accept you as my wife and treat you as a valued member of the family, we will move from St. Joe and set up a jewelry and watch repair shop as far away as necessary. I won't put up with you being treated as she has been treating you."

"Oh, Will, no. It's so very hard to leave family, I know. Patrick and I did just that."

"I know. I hope it won't be necessary, but I will do so. My grandfather moved from Bavaria to America, maybe not for the same reasons, but he was able to start in a new country. We would only be starting in a new state. I won't have her making your life miserable."

"I haven't been miserable."

Will kissed her nose. "You are a terrible liar. I've noticed your moods lately and wondered if it was something I was doing that was making you so somber and nervous. Now, I know it was Mother being a harridan. I'm sorry you had to be subject to her attitude. It won't happen again. But, Pearl…" Will stroked her cheek. "You will tell me if she ever says or does anything that makes you uncomfortable or feel bad in any way. No more hiding it from me."

When she glanced away, Will placed his fingers on her chin, gently forcing her to look at him. "Promise me."

Pearl searched his face, her eyes darting back and forth as she studied him. "I promise. I just don't want her to hold this against me."

"If she does, she will be forcing us to move. I will close the shop and leave town in a heartbeat. You are more important to me than anything else, even my family."

Tears slipped from Pearl's eyes as he spoke. Will leaned in and gave her a gentle kiss, then held her against him as she wept.

Lillian was fixing her lunch when she heard footsteps coming up the stairs. Or rather, stomping up the stairs. She left the kitchen and saw her mother storm into the parlor. The look on her face indicated there was a problem. Inwardly, Lillian flinched. This wasn't good.

"You will never believe what your brother just did. He threw me, his mother, out of his house and told me not to return."

Uh oh. "What happened, Mother?"

Luella flopped down on the davenport. "He just told me I couldn't come."

"Mother, Will wouldn't simply banish you without giving a reason." Lillian saw a flush rise on her mother's face. "So, what was the reason?" She sat down beside her.

"I was only trying to help. Will deserves to have a wife who knows how to maintain a proper home."

"Pearl is very accomplished at homemaking. More so than me."

"You manage well, Lillian. I know what you are capable of."

"There's the key, Mother. I'm capable, but don't really care if it's all done properly. Pearl does. She kept this place spotless even though she was working full-time. She's a good cook, too. I'm surprised Will hasn't gained weight since they've been married." She could see her words weren't making her mother feel any better. "What did you say to make him so angry he doesn't want you around?"

Luella sat silently picking at lint on her skirt.

"Mother, do you think Will is a success? A man who is able to run this business well?"

Luella looked up, startled. "Yes, of course."

"Do you trust he's an adult who can handle the challenges of life?"

"Yes."

"Then why don't you trust that he would know what's

best for himself?"

"What do you mean? What's best for him?"

"Or maybe the better question is: Who is best for him? Pearl is devoted to Will. And I don't think it's all gratitude either."

"How can it be anything other than gratitude? She married him so she'd be supported."

"True, he asked her to marry him so she and her baby would be taken care of. But he also loves her. You only have to see how he looks as her and how he treats her. All that really happened was the timetable was moved up. Instead of him asking her to marry him next summer, he asked her this summer. It was going to happen."

"How do you know? Maybe he would have changed his mind."

"You weren't around. You didn't see him around her like I did. He's in love with her and that's not going to change."

"But she doesn't love him and she has that baby coming."

"Is that what bothers you? The baby. It's not as if she's a fallen woman. She's a widow. There's no shame in that."

"But the shop…"

"Is just a business. I know the history and tradition. I know that means a lot to you. It does to me, and to Will, too. But what's more important? The tradition or Will being happy and married to the woman he loves?"

Luella looked out the window across the room, avoiding the question.

"I think Pearl does love him. She's not ready to admit it, maybe doesn't even realize she does. It's not been very long since her first husband died.

"You do know she didn't jump at the chance to marry him. He had to convince her. She didn't want him to be bound to a woman then find someone else he would love. Will told her that no matter what, he would honor their covenant. They plan to live a Biblical marriage."

"So she's going to submit to him?" Luella looked at Lillian.

"Will plans to place her first and be a husband who supports her and sacrifices for her, making sure she's without spot or wrinkle, nourishing and tenderly caring for her, just as Christ does the church. That's a much higher calling than submitting. If he does that, she won't have difficulty allowing him to be the head of the house.

"Mother, you and Father taught us how to live fruitful lives, dependent only on God and what you taught us. Will is doing that. Doing that with Pearl. She's good for him. She is what has made him really settle into the business. Until Pearl, Will was only doing the job. Now, he's committed and passionate about his work. Pearl is the seal on all your teaching. You and Father taught him how to love his wife. To give of himself selflessly. Let him."

Luella pulled a lace-edged handkerchief from her sleeve and wiped her cheeks. "Pearl sent me this handkerchief while we were in Hot Springs." Luella was silent for several minutes then she sighed. "*'For this reason a man will leave his father and mother and be joined to his wife, and the two will become one flesh.'* Maybe that's what I have fought against so hard. Will has always looked to me as the woman in his life. Now he has Pearl. I do like her, have since that first day. It was just so hard to see him turning to another woman." Luella turned tear-filled eyes toward Lillian. "Do you think she'll ever forgive me?"

"I think you'll find Pearl to be a very forgiving person. Tell her what you were struggling with. Explain it all. Confess is the word I'm sure fits in this case."

Luella nodded. Lillian placed her arms around her mother and hugged her.

CHAPTER SIXTEEN

Will shut the cash register drawer, thanking the customer for their purchase. The woman had bought a lace collar Pearl had crocheted. Placing several collars she had considered back in the display case, he ran his finger over the ones Pearl had made.

The celebration supper had turned out well, even with the problems of the day caused by his mother. He and Pearl had eaten lunch and then taken a nap, the emotions of the morning having taken their toll. Will was concerned that the stress Pearl had been under as his mother spent days criticizing everything she did would affect the baby and her in a negative way. He'd even made her change into her nightgown so she would be more comfortable as she napped. Of course, he'd had an ulterior motive for that decision. Will was glad she'd been enthusiastic about his idea when she woke.

Will wished Pearl had told him what his mother had been doing. She never would have though. The guilt she took upon herself over his parents' reaction to their marriage prevented her ever mentioning a problem with them.

She also carried a burden his confession of love had placed on her shoulders. Her reaction of 'Oh, Will' had been filled with so many emotions; grief, despair, hope, longing, and maybe a tiny bit of reciprocation of love. Maybe he was projecting his desire for Pearl to love him into her words. Daily, Will prayed for her to move passed her mourning for Patrick and begin to feel a greater affection for himself. The way his mother had been treating Pearl certainly didn't help.

Will shook the tension from his shoulders as the shop door opened. Seeing who entered tightened them up again — his mother. He let out his breath in a soft sigh. Just what he needed to start his week off on the wrong foot.

Pearl and he had gone to church, even sitting with the rest of his family. Pearl had been pale and stiff, twisting her handkerchief until he'd laid his hand over hers in her lap not caring if anyone else saw. She needed his support more than keeping up proper decorum. They'd begged off going to his parents' house for Sunday dinner with the rest of the family. They had just said Pearl was tired, implying it was her condition. They'd gone to a diner for dinner then home. Although spending Sundays with family occurred every week, Will enjoyed having the day of rest with only Pearl. He planned to do so at least once a month, if they ever went back to joining the rest of his family for the afternoon.

Will stood to greet Luella. "Good morning, Mother." He gave her a light kiss on her cheek then sat back down. Turning back to the workbench, he picked up the watch he'd been working on when the customer came into the shop.

"Will, we missed you yesterday. You and Pearl," Luella said.

"Pearl was tired. We thought it best she rested at our home." He focused on the watch, not looking at her as she sat in the other swiveling desk chair.

Silence hung like a heavy curtain between them. As much as he loved his mother, Will couldn't act as if nothing was wrong between them. Pearl was his wife and deserved his support.

"Will… Um… I…" Luella stammered.

He remained silent working on the watch.

"Will, I've thought a great deal about why I was being so very hard on Pearl. I was totally in the wrong and I'm sorry."

The words came out in a rush. He looked at her but didn't say anything.

"I will say I was shocked to learn of your marriage. I'd seen your interest in Pearl before we left on our trip. You remember I warned you, no, that's the wrong word. I mentioned my concern over your attraction to her. My concern wasn't disapproving of Pearl. It was because she was grieving and had an entire year of mourning to get through. I didn't want you to be hurt if you pinned your hopes on her only to have Pearl not return your affections. I took that out on her at that time too, which was wrong of me. It wasn't her. She's a wonderful young woman. It's me."

Luella took a deep breath and pulled her handkerchief from her sleeve. "Pearl sent me this while we were in Hot Springs. I know she realized I was treating her poorly before we left. I know she couldn't figure out why I suddenly was treating her like a pariah. Still, she wrote about the lacework she was doing and her excitement about the wedding gown. She thanked me several times for helping her get the commissions and for how well her lace was selling. This handkerchief was a small token of her gratitude." She spread the cotton square with its wide lace border on the tabletop, smoothing it with her hand.

"If she hadn't been in mourning, I might have endorsed your interest in her. But then, again, maybe not." Luella's shoulders sagged. "I realized after you banished me from your house what my real issue was. I was jealous of her. Jealous that she was replacing me as the most important woman in your life. If you married her, you wouldn't need me anymore."

"Mother, Pearl isn't replacing you. You'll always be my

mother. She's my wife."

"I know, but you'll always be my little boy."

Will took her hand in his. Softly, he said, "I haven't been your little boy for a number of years now. I'm a grown man. I've worked in this shop since I was in my mid-teens. Now, with Father's health not good, I run it. I'm building on the legacy Grandfather started and Father built on.

"You and he raised me to be self-reliant. I'm able to manage my life successfully because of what you both taught and all the support you gave me. I'll be forever grateful for it all. Now, my life includes another woman who isn't replacing you. She adds to the richness of my life.

"Mother, she's a good woman, talented and sweet. She never mentioned how you were treating her. I had no idea. It hurt me more than you can know to see the first woman I ever loved, who is the example of the type of woman I wanted for a wife, being so critical and hurtful of the woman I love."

Tears slipped down Luella's cheeks. "Pearl never said one word back to me whenever I criticized her. She welcomed me into your home each day, going about her chores while I commented on every little thing she did differently than I do."

Repentance was flowing from his mother. "What do you want to do?"

"I'd like to go and beg Pearl's forgiveness. I understand that she might not want to, or to allow me to come for visits, but I need to tell her how sorry I am."

Will stood and drew his mother into a hug. "I think you'll find that Pearl is a very forgiving person."

"I hope so Will. I never wanted to drive you and her away."

"We don't want to be driven away, either."

~~~~~

Will and Luella had to wait until Lillian returned from the errands she was running before they could leave the shop. When they arrived at home, Pearl was in the kitchen, elbow deep in the washtub. The lines behind the house were full of clothing and sheets. Pearl's forehead was shiny with sweat, her expression cautiously welcoming as she dried her hands and smoothed her damp apron.

"Good morning. May I get you some coffee or raspberry water?"

"No, thank you," Luella said.

Will moved to Pearl. "Come, let's go into the parlor. It's a little steamy in here."

Pearl searched his eyes as she untied her apron and lifted a hand to tuck a strand of hair behind her ear. "Okay."

Pearl sat on the edge of the settee and Will slid in beside her. Luella took the sewing chair across the coffee table from them and cleared her throat.

"Pearl, I want to tell you how sorry I am about how I've been treating you. I was wrong and should never have criticized you for doing things differently than I do. You're an accomplished homemaker. I know that, and knew it even as I was making my comments. I was jealous of you becoming such an important person in Will's life. I hope you can forgive me."

"Of course, I forgive you."

Will could see an uncertain hope come into his mother's eyes.

"Pearl, could we start over? I've let my jealousy damage the friendship we were developing. I hope it's not too late to become friends. I'll mind my tongue and help any way I can." Luella grinned. "I may not always succeed. I want you to let me know when I cross the line."

Pearl reached across the space between them. Luella clasped her hand. "I'd love to forget the difficulties and renew our friendship."

Will saw the affection they had for each other peek out from where it had been hiding in both of the women he loved so much.

"Is there anything I can do to help you prepare for the baby? I think I'm a pretty good grandmother, and I want to be for your child, too." Luella squeezed Pearl's hand a couple of times.

Pearl surprised both Will and Luella when she burst into tears. Will gathered his wife into his arms comforting her, looking to his mother for help. Luella came over and patted Pearl on the back for comfort.

When she'd calmed, Pearl took a shuddery breath and said, "I've been praying we could have a better relationship. I'm so afraid of giving birth. I've felt so alone, without any family. Lillian isn't able to help with this. I so wanted you to be willing to help. I'm afraid I'll be a terrible mother. I don't know enough about what babies need."

Luella pushed Will away and sat beside Pearl. She hugged her then took Pearl's face between her hands, looking into her eyes. "You'll be a wonderful mother. And, babies only need three things: Love, food and to be warm and dry. But mostly they need love. You have that in abundance. And if you need some help in that department, just call me and I'll be there to give that little one more love than he can hold."

~~~~~

Pearl bit her lip as she rolled out the dough for Mother Lee's Rolls. The pumpkin and mince meat pies were in the oven baking. She would form the rolls and let them rise. They'd be baked just before she and Will left to go to his parents' house for Thanksgiving.

For the past two months Pearl had been cautiously allowing her relationship with Luella to grow. She'd been wary at first that her mother-in-law would again begin to treat her with disrespect. The caring, giving woman whom

Pearl had met in late April, who had been replaced by the critical one of the summer and early fall was back, much to Pearl's delight.

Being alone in a new city, having her husband die, then finding the generous Miller family had done much to soothe the grieving young woman. When Luella's attitude had changed it had brought more sadness to an already discouraged Pearl.

She'd known Luella wouldn't welcome Pearl and Will's marriage. The vehemence with which Luella had expressed her objection had surprised and distressed Pearl. She'd reacted in the only way she thought might soothe Luella. She'd simply accepted the criticism and done the best she could, keeping silent about it all to Will. The last thing she'd wanted was to become more of an obstacle between him and his parents.

With the friendship between Luella and Pearl growing, her focus shifted to her feelings toward Will. He was so very loving toward her, taking care of her even more tenderly as her pregnancy progressed.

He'd insisted she see a doctor to make sure everything was normal and she was healthy. Pearl had objected to having Vernon Strasser as her physician. He was a friend and the possibility of him attending the baby's birth simply didn't bring comfort to the expectant mother. Vernon had understood and recommended a colleague whom Pearl accepted. She hoped to give birth at home, but in the event of complications she was comfortable with this man's skills.

Will had surprised her in late October when he came home driving a red Model T automobile. He'd purchased the 1909 model from Mr. Norbury who was purchasing a new 1911 Maxwell. Now, he'd come home daily for lunch and take her back to the shop for the afternoon. Not having to ride the trolley was wonderful, but Pearl wondered how well the automobile would run in the winter.

Pearl dipped the last roll in melted butter and folded the circle over laying it in the pan. She covered all the pans with a clean dish towel, noting the time so she would know when to bake them after they'd risen. The pies were done so she removed them from the oven and placed them on racks on the table to cool. Removing her apron, Pearl left the kitchen. She needed to talk with Will and now was as good a time as any.

Will was seated at the desk in the corner of the parlor. He spent many of his hours at home designing jewelry. The commission pieces for Mr. Norbury had brought many new customers into the shop who wanted one-of-a-kind items for their wives or themselves. The money these wealthy people were willing to spend astounded Pearl. She'd had several commissions for lacework also. She wasn't taking new orders for complicated pieces as she knew her time would be more limited once the baby was born.

Smiling at the jewelry periodicals scattered on the coffee table and floor, Pearl picked them up, stacking them together on the table. Will and Lillian shared a trait. They weren't overly concerned with keeping their home neat. Pearl didn't mind. Will was so caring, she'd pick up after him as much as was needed.

Walking up behind him, Pearl slipped her hands over his shoulders and down his chest, leaning against him as close as her belly would permit. "What are you working on?"

Will straightened and lifted a hand to place it over hers. "It's a choker necklace of platinum, diamonds and pearls. This will be the style of the earrings too." He pointed to the drops of pearls suspended from the diamond encrusted chain.

"Lovely."

"Would you like something like this for yourself?"

"No. I'd rather you spend your time making them to sell. I…"

Just then the baby kicked straight out, bumping against the back of Will's head. He jerked around, his eyes wide with wonder.

"Wow! That was some kick. Do you need to sit down?" Will stood and led her to the settee.

Pearl smiled. "No, I'm fine, but I will sit with you." She patted the space beside her. Now that it was time, she found she was nervous and tongue-tied. She could feel her cheeks heating and looked down at their clasped hands.

"Pearl, is everything all right? You seem distressed or worried." Will squeezed her hand causing her to look at his face.

She studied him, seeing his silvery blue eyes filled with concern. His blonde hair was mussed from his fingers running through it as he worked out a design. She knew he thought his nose was too big, and maybe it was, but she thought it gave his face character.

Pearl laid her hand on his cheek. "Everything is wonderful. I know you've been worried because I've been quiet lately. I've been trying to figure out how to tell you. What words to use."

The anxiety in his eyes grew. This was what she'd wanted to avoid, yet she'd caused it with her dithering.

"Will, don't fret. I just wanted everything to be perfect. I wanted to do something special for you, but haven't been able to think of a way that would mean something to you. I decided today was the day.

"You've been so very good to me from the moment we met. I was at my lowest, not knowing if I would survive through the week until I was paid. You came to my rescue." She waved away his protest when he started to object. "Yes, I know Lillian and your mother were involved. You, though, stood out to me with your support. You befriended me. Allowed Lillian to kick you out of the apartment so I could move in." They both smiled at the memory of her machinations in getting him to buy the house.

"You made such a great sacrifice for me when you found out I was expecting and asked me to marry you. Don't say you didn't." She held up her hand to stop him from speaking.

"You've honored the Biblical verses about marriage in so many ways. Through it all you've honored my mourning for Patrick.

"I went to his grave the other day. I needed to tell him about you. Needed to tell him I and his baby are going to be okay. That I've found a wonderful man to raise it. To be the father he never had the chance to be. To let him know we have found a family here who will love us.

"I also needed to tell him I've found someone. Someone I love with all my heart the way I loved him. Because, Will, I do love you. I…"

The rest of the words were swallowed in Will's kiss. Or rather kisses.

"I've longed for you to say those words," Will said when they finally came up for air. "I've loved you for so long. I think ever since you fainted in my shop." He kissed her again.

"I love you. It's taken me longer to realize it. I can't say when it began or even when I finally knew. I just did. You became the most important person in my life. The one I want to be with. The one whom God gave me to love and cherish. My Will." She kissed him softly.

"I like that; being yours. I'll be Pearl's Will for as long as I live." His kiss was filled with desire. He glanced at the clock. "I think we have time to celebrate before we go to Mother's, don't you?" He stood and pulled Pearl to her feet and led the way to the bedroom.

~~~~~

"Come on, Will. Hurry, we are late enough. Hand me the basket. You take the pie carrier." Pearl stood by the automobile, bouncing slightly on her toes. She glanced at the house as Will did as instructed.

"Relax, they won't start eating without us."

"I know, but I don't like being late, especially for the reason we are. What if they ask why? What do we tell them?"

He grinned at her as they hurried up the walk. "The truth?"

"Heaven's no, Will. How embarrassing."

"We can blame your condition. You needed to lie down for a while this morning, and that I made you stay in bed longer than I should have."

"Will, really," Pearl objected.

"That we needed to celebrate your love for me?" Will's eyes sparkled with love and mischief.

"You are not helping." Pearl tried to suppress her grin but failed.

Several nieces and nephews met them at the door, excited to see them.

"Grandma's been wondering where you were. Grandpa said it's to be expected of newlyweds but wouldn't explain what he meant by that." Mary's eldest daughter said as she held the door open so they could enter the house.

"We're hungry," Josey's four-year-old son said. Several other heads nodded.

Pearl shot an exasperated look at Will. "We're sorry. I'm sure you are. I've made plenty of rolls. Here, this will tide you over." She flipped the towel covering the basket back and handed a roll to each child. They all grinned their thanks and ran off to let the others see their bounty and know that Uncle Will and Aunt Pearl were finally here.

The kitchen was a flurry of activity when they entered.

Luella greeted them with quick kisses on the cheek and orders to help get everything on the table. Pearl was glad to comply since it meant not having to explain their tardiness.

Matthew stood at the head of the table, the large platters of turkey and ham in front of him. As he gave thanks Will grasped Pearl's hand under the table, giving it a squeeze. She smiled. Eight months ago, she had been overcome with grief, struggling to survive. Now, she was part of a loving family, waiting for her child to be born in the next month, being loved by a wonderful man, and loving him in return. She had doubted God's will for her back then. Now, she knew Will had been His will for her. Pearl gave her own thanks as she squeezed his hand in return.

CHAPTER SEVENTEEN

"Will." Pearl poked him in the side. He grunted in his sleep and turned over. "Will." She poked him again.

"What?" he mumbled. "It's still dark. Too early to get up."

"It's the baby. It's time."

"That's nice. Go back to sleep." Will pulled the covers up over his shoulder.

Pearl flipped hers away and got out of bed. A contraction made her stand still for a few moments then she turned on the small lamp on the bedside table. She needed to see the clock so she could time the contractions.

Will sat up in bed suddenly, eyes wide. "What? The baby? Now?" He jumped out of bed and grabbed his trousers, putting them on over his pajamas. "Should you be out of bed? You need to lie down." He hurried around the bed and tried to make her get back in.

"No, Will. I have things to do. Maybe I should have just let you sleep, but I needed to be able to see the clock." Pearl pulled the blankets down to the end of the bed and got the bundle of towels and sheets to place on it. "This baby is finally going to make its appearance. A New Year's baby."

"I'll go get the water boiling." Will rushed out of the room.

While he was gone Pearl had another contraction. Four minutes apart. She was trying to remain calm. Will was nervous enough. He had been getting more so daily as they waited for the baby to arrive. She thought he might fall in a heap if she revealed how nervous she was.

Pearl looked out the window and breathed a sigh of relief. There wasn't any new snow. There'd been a thaw over the last few days and much of it had melted. Will could take the automobile and get Luella.

"The water is on the stove. What should I do now? Do you need to lie down?" Will ran a hand through his hair making it stand on end.

"Will you drive over and get your mother, please? I don't want her to have to walk. I'll telephone while you head over."

"And leave you alone? Are you kidding?" Will paced back and forth in the room.

"You want me to go with you?"

He stopped and looked at her in shock. "No, you shouldn't be out on a night like this."

"It actually looks quite nice out. There's a moon and no wind. I don't think it is icy. And it's morning; five-thirty." Another contraction. Pearl bent over, clutching her belly. When it passed, she looked at Will. "Please, go get your mother. I really need her with me."

He'd gone white watching her deal with the labor pain. Without a word, he rushed to put on socks and shoes, ran out, and grabbed his coat off the hook. "You call and we'll be back as soon as possible." The door slammed as he ran from the house.

Now that she was alone, fear nearly paralyzed her. Pearl let out a breath and wiped her hand down her face. She went to the kitchen and turned the crank on the phone. It took two more times of cranking before the operator asked for the number.

Pearl didn't think anyone would ever answer. Finally, Matthew answered. "Hello?" The voice was sleep-filled and groggy.

"Matthew, this is Pearl. Will's on his way over in the motorcar. The baby is on its way. Would Luella please come over?"

"Oh, of course. Wonderful." He sounded wide awake now. "She's already getting dressed. When the telephone rang, she said it was most likely you. We'll be there as soon as possible. You relax. Everything will be fine. Luella told me to tell you that. You better do as you're told, young lady. Relax."

Pearl chuckled. "Yes, sir. You tell her I am obeying, at least to the best of my ability. I'll do better when she's here."

"I'm sure. We'll be there shortly. Good-bye."

Pearl hung up the earphone and went to check the water. She grinned. Will had put the water on the stove but not added any fuel. She stirred up the coals and bent over adding more. As she stood, closing the door, water ran down her legs, pooling on the floor.

Another contraction kept her standing there, clutching the table with one hand the stove handle with the other. Pearl prayed Will would drive safely but get back with Luella very soon.

She changed into a clean dry gown and was on her knees mopping up the floor when the kitchen door opened and Will ran in.

"What are you doing on the floor?"

"Washing it."

"What?" Will fairly shrieked. "Now's not the time to wash the floor."

"It's all right, Will," Luella said, coming up behind him. "Did your water break, dear?" She was taking off her coat.

Pearl allowed Will to help her stand. She was glad for the assistance since she wasn't sure she'd be able to get up on her own. "Yes." Another contraction hit taking her breath. They were getting stronger.

As soon as it eased, Will scooped her up in his arms and strode into the bedroom, placing her gently on the bed. "You stay here. I'll finish in the kitchen."

"That's a good idea, Will," Luella said, pushing him gently from the room. "You make coffee and make sure your father has a cup. Maybe make him some toast too. You know how growly he gets if he doesn't eat soon after he wakes up." She closed the door, leaving him on the other side.

Luella turned around and smiled at Pearl. "Hopefully that will keep him occupied until Matthew can calm him down. Otherwise he'll pester us to no end. Now, you and I are going to have a baby."

~~~~~

Will stood looking at the closed door to his bedroom. Something told him he wasn't welcome in there right now. A hand patted his shoulder.

"Let's go get that floor cleaned," his father said. "Then let's make coffee."

"Mother told me I need to feed you too. You get growly if you don't eat."

Matthew laughed. "She's right, but she says that when she wants the fathers-to-be out of the way. She's not only helped with our seven, soon to be eight, grandchildren's births, but many others in the neighborhood. She's sort of an unofficial midwife for this part of St. Joe." At Will's shocked look Matthew continued. "You didn't know that, did you? Not something she shares with many. Your mother's a talented, giving woman, but she's also rather private about her skills."

Will filled the coffee percolator basket with grounds and fit it into the pot. "We'll have coffee soon. Would you like breakfast?"

"You cooking it?"

"Yes."

"Not really sure. Can you cook?" Matthew's eyes twinkled.

They chatted while Will fried bacon, then eggs and made toast. When Will put the filled plates on the table and sat down, Matthew said grace.

"Will," Matthew said, "I want to tell you, I think you made a good decision."

Will looked at his father after taking his first bite.

"About marrying Pearl. You made a good choice. I said when we talked right after your mother and I returned from Hot Springs that time would tell. Well, what I've observed over the past months has shown me you made a good choice.

"Pearl is a lovely woman inside and out. She handled how your mother treated her with grace, although I think she should have told her to butt out. But then, I'm not the new daughter-in-law trying to find approval.

"I just want you to know, I'm proud of you. I love Pearl as if she was my own daughter. This baby will be my, our, grandchild just as the others are. If it's a boy and he wants the shop, then it should go to him. You were right when you said it was tradition not law.

"I want to make sure you knew how proud I am of you and how much I love you. You're a good man, Will Miller."

Will had to swallow the lump in his throat before he could speak. "Thank you, Father. It means a lot to me for you to say that. I had a good example to follow. I just hope I'm half as good a father as mine has been."

"I've no doubt you'll be twice as good."

~~~~~

Will sat down heavily on the settee when a scream came from the bedroom. "Is that supposed to happen?" He turned worried eyes toward his father.

"Usually does. Luella hasn't come out asking that we call a doctor, so I'd say things are going well. May not be

187

long now."

Another scream came, longer than the first. Will sank back leaning against the back of the settee. He looked at the grandmother clock on the wall as it chimed the hour. After the short tune it bonged ten times. "Does it usually take this long?"

"This is short compared to some Luella's attended. But Pearl didn't let anyone know until she was pretty far along. Some want her there as soon as the pains start. That makes it a long, long wait."

No more sound came from the bedroom. "Shouldn't we hear a cry?" Will was worried.

His father didn't say anything which was an answer in itself.

When the bedroom door opened, both men stood. Luella came out, smiling. "Go meet your daughter, Will. Mama and baby are both doing well."

Matthew slapped Will on the back. "Congratulations."

Will ran into the bedroom. Pearl was lying against a bunch of pillows, the wrapped bundle in her arms.

"Isn't she beautiful, Will?" Pearl beamed.

The baby's face was red and seemed squashed. It didn't matter. She was beautiful. Will leaned down and kissed Pearl. "Yes, she's beautiful."

"She has ten fingers and toes. I counted."

"How are you?" Will touched the baby's cheek. The little mouth opened turning toward the touch.

"I'm well, tired but well."

"So, we have little Patricia Luella here."

"Yes. I haven't told your mother yet."

"She'll be pleased."

Pearl yawned. "I'm very tired."

"I'll get the proud grandparents and we can introduce Patty to them. Then we'll leave you to sleep."

Pearl smiled and nodded.

When Matthew and Luella stood at the end of the bed,

Will picked up his daughter. "I'd like you to meet Patricia Luella Miller. She's named after two people Pearl loves very much."

Tears streamed down Luella's face. "Thank you, Pearl. I don't deserve the honor."

Will saw Pearl smile as her eyes closed. "Let's go and get acquainted with little Patty and let her mama sleep for a while."

"Will," Pearl called softly.

He turned back and went to her. "Yes?"

"Thank you for being my Will. I love you."

He kissed her gently. "I love you too, my Pearl."

~oOoOo~

Thank you for reading
Pearl's Will

Each book in the
Lockets & Lace
series is a Clean, Sweet Western Historical Romance.
You may find all the books in this series as they are
published by searching for
"**Lockets and Lace**" on **Amazon.com**
Please follow this series' page to be notified when new
books in the Sweethearts of Jubilee Springs and other
series books written by
Sweet Americana authors become available.

If you enjoyed this book, please help other readers find
it by leaving a review on
Amazon Review
and
Goodreads.
Just a few words will do. Reviews make *all* the
difference!

To learn more about the Sweet Americana
Sweethearts blog, our authors, and our individual books,
please visit
SweetAmericanaSweethearts.blogspot.com

Lockets & Lace books
by
Sweet Americana Sweethearts
Blog Authors:

~o0o~

0.0

The Bavarian Jeweler by Zina Abbott

The Lockets & Lace series prequel:
Sent to America in 1849 to avoid inscription into
the Bavarian army preparing for war against Prussia,
Wilhelm Mueller, a master jeweler and watchmaker, goes
with his father's promise that he will always have a little
touch of Bavaria with him. His British cabin mate on the
ship who knows German helps him learn English. He
meets some of his fellow passengers, including a group of
Irish refugees escaping the potato famine. The lace made
by a certain young woman captures Wilhelm's attention as
much as her pretty face and curly hair.
Upon landing in New Orleans, he finds
everything is new in his adopted country, including his
name. After sailing by steamboat up the Mississippi River,
he stops at what was in 1850 the crossroads of America. It
is there he holds to a touch of his homeland by opening his
Bavarian Jewelry and Watch Repair shop. Over the
decades, as he becomes know for a particular kind of
jewelry, he realizes he has gained more by coming to
America than what he left behind.

1.

Oregon Dreams by Patricia PacJac Carroll

Hope Castleberry lives with her aunt and uncle and their two daughters. While an infant, Hope's mother died, and her father dropped her off at his uncle's and went on to Oregon. Now, Hope is grown and wants to find her father. The only thing she has to remind her of him is a locket and a piece of lace from her mother's wedding dress. Since a young child, she's wanted to go west and find her father and settle in the new land.

Darren Thorsten has dreamed of going west to Oregon ever since an old trapper told him of the delightful land. He has plans to marry and get acreage by homesteading with a company that is leaving early in April. He'll have to find a wife. But how hard can that be. He's a good looking, strong man with big dreams. His family decided to go back to Norway.

His mother's only plea was for him to marry a Scandinavian girl with blonde hair and blue eyes. Darren agreed. After all, there had to be plenty of blondes scattered throughout the country.

His first stop in Quiet, Missouri proves him right. But the two blonde women are already spoken for. Yet, they tell him there is a third daughter.

Hope comes bounding into the house and Darren's heart is taken. Only one small matter, she has dark hair and brown eyes.

Hope and Darren's trails collide on the journey to Oregon. Can her past and his old ways give in to bridge a path for their future?

2.

Silent Harmony by Caryl McAdoo

Harmony is a 4-yr-old deaf girl, the niece of my heroine Melody Parker. There are 3 Parker sisters who lost their father and Lucy, the oldest's, husband when they perished in the Civil War. My hero is coming from Great Lakes area to DeKalb TX (near where the Parker sisters live) to open a school for the deaf--His mother's brother offered the old homeplace for his school. She dies abruptly on the way. Then traveling on alone, hero's robbed and beaten and left for dead. The thieves took his mother's locket that his dad had given her. Hero's only photographs of them. It turns up in the Bavarian Jewelry & Watch Repair shop in St. Joseph, Missouri.

3.

Otto's Offer by Zina Abbott

In 1868, Otto Atwell has a 160 acre homestead near Abilene, Kansas and a limp as a result of a Cheyenne musket ball hitting his lower back while with the 16th Kansas Volunteer Cavalry on the Powder River Expedition in 1865. What he didn't have was a wife. Then again, what woman would want to marry a cripple?

Libby Jones comes to Junction City as a mail order bride. Not only does the man who sent for her reject her, he tries to sell her to the local brothel to recoup his fee. Otto offers to marry her, but she rejects him in favor of a job with his relatives.

Will Otto's offer still stand when trouble from Libby's past catches up with her?

4.

Melly Unyielding

by Abagail Eldan

Melly is a woman with secrets. Thatcher is the man with enough patience to unlock them.

For fifteen years, Carmella Harperson's life has been confined to a couple of acres in the middle of a large forest. She's alive but hopeless, each day a struggle.

William Thatcher Rainer's past haunts him as he hunts down the man who destroyed his life. His days are filled with memories of the carnage of war; his nights with nightmares of the death of his wife.

On the road, to find the man responsible for the misery of so many, they must work together and learn to trust.

Neither is prepared for what they find at the end of their journey.

5.

Locket Full of Love by Heather Blanton

In 1867 Juliet Watts and her husband Hugh are caught up in a vicious Indian raid. On the verge of escaping, though, Hugh realizes Juliet is not wearing a locket he gave her. Risking his life, he heads back to their home to retrieve it and stubborn Juliet follows. Both are captured and Hugh is killed. Juliet survives but now despises the locket and wants nothing else to do with it. She also harbors a deep sense of betrayal with Hugh and God over the whole event. Robert Hall, the young soldier who saved her, however, promises to hang on to the locket in case she ever wants it back. Ten years later, Juliet and Robert meet again in St. Joe, MO where Juliet runs a saloon. He gives her back the locket and she accidentally discovers a secret compartment, but not one easily opened. A trip to the Bavarian Jeweler reveals that Hugh was keeping secrets. A key hidden in the locket starts Juliet and Robert on a journey of mystery and discovery. The closer she gets to the truth about her dead husband, the closer she gets to untangling the lies surrounding Robert. Will her heart survive the revelations?

6.

Tending Trouble by Linda Carroll-Bradd

Traveling west to become a mail-order bride is the most adventurous act Bostonian Imogene Franklin ever did. Unfortunately, the groom chose another so now Imogene must make her way on her own. Dreading the idea of returning home to continue raising her siblings, she is reduced to waiting tables in the Dorado café.

Guilt hangs heavy over Reggie Othmann—ever since he brought home a childhood illness that claimed both his parents' lives. The ink is barely dry on Reggie's degree when he arrives home in Dorado to establish a medical practice. All he's wanted since he was ten years old is to help people, but the townspeople have been without a doctor for so long, they don't flock through his doors as expected.

An illness sweeps the town, and Reggie is overwhelmed, fearing he's not qualified to heal them. Imogene steps in and together, they work hard to prevent anyone from dying, spending days together. Is their emotional tie born of the closeness of the ordeal or perhaps something more?

7.

Chasing a Chance by Angela Raines

Edwin 'Win' Markum has loved Mary Winters since they were children. When she married another, Win left to make his way in the world. Now, through a chance encounter with an old friend, Win learns that Mary is a widow and living in a town that has been overrun with an outlaw gang. He leaves his business and heads out to help Mary, for he has never stopped loving her and carries the locket he bought for her as a reminder of that love.

8.

Disarming Amy by Sandra E Sinclair

Amy Wheeler has her life mapped out. She'll marry her fiancé, move east and start her new life in Maine. The secret contained in the belly of a fish will halt those well thought out plans, and change the course of her life.

Eugene Collart is an obedient son, and sole heir to a growing dynasty. The problem is, the things his father wants for him, are at odds with what he wants. If Eugene wants to live a life governed by his own rules, and go against his controlling father's wishes, he must strike out and find his own way in life.

Fate throws these two together. Their futures are aligned but sparks fly, antipathy grows, and emotions run high as they are thrust unwillingly into each other's lives.

Complications mount up. Eugene and Amy fight their attraction for each other amidst the animosity and burning passion raging between them.

9.

Pearl's Will by Sophie Dawson

Will Miller doesn't know what to think when the lovely young woman faints in his jewelry and watch repair shop-- except he wants to help her any way he can. Widow Pearl Ward, struggling to survive, needs to sell the watch-locket given to her on her eighteenth birthday. When he learns she's expecting, he proposes. Will Pearl's feelings for her late husband stand between them? Can they build a life together with his mother dead set against them?

Books By Sophie Dawson
Cottonwood Series
Healing Love
Lord's Love
Giving Love
Redeeming Love (With George McVey)
Stones Creek Series
Leah's Peace
Chasing Norie
Chloe's Choice (Short Story)
Chloe's Sanctuary
Stones Creek Ladies Of Sanctuary House
Laundry Lady's Love
Music of Her Heart
Love's Infestation
Mold and Marriage
Spots Before Marriage
Mice and Marriage
Single Books
Seeing The Life
Rescued By Love
Java Cupid Multi-Author series
Java Priority #4
Java Protect #10

If you enjoyed this book and would like to find other great Christian Indie Authors reads, follow the link below. Christian Books in Multiple Genres, Join Christian Indie Author ~ Readers Group on Facebook. Opportunities for free books and giveaways.